Table of C

To my neice, Ivy, and her parents, Kat and Ama.
Thank you for inspiring me to write this story.

Skull Daddy

Skull Daddy, Skull Daddy, what do you see? What does the future hold for me?

Skull Daddy, Skull Daddy, what do you hear? Is it a friend or a foe that is near?

Skull Daddy, Skull Daddy, is it the time? The moment for me to claim what is mine?

April

Jade gripped the sides of her coffee cup like she was trying to keep it from falling apart. The drink was long since cold, but her fingers burned all the same. All she wanted was to retreat to her bed, forget any of this was happening.

Something in her wife's eyes made her afraid to ask – Cass was past her breaking point – but Jade had to know.

"Is it...?"

Jade thought her voice sounded too small. It wasn't strong enough to continue the thought. She couldn't tell whether Cass heard her or not. Cass was so still, Jade couldn't tell if she was breathing. A dewy buildup of saliva had gathered at the edge of her cracked lips, threatening to spill over. Her eyes focused somewhere else even as they pointed in the direction of the phone. She was nothing more than an empty shell.

Cass uttered a few halting words through her numb lips.

"It's my mom. She, uh..."

As Cass clenched her phone, Jade expected shards of glass and plastic to explode out of her wife's grip. A mental image that Jade couldn't shake away. A sliver of the screen lodged in Cass's throat, another in her left eye sticking out of her shattered glasses. Jade was sticky with a layer of blood that wasn't there.

"They found her car," said Cass after a long, trembling sigh. "In a ditch."

Jade blinked, and the blood left her vision. Cass was fine, but only just. Her face was an ashy grey, and for the first time in their marriage, Jade saw the ghost of wrinkles on her wife's skin. Had those always been there? Or had the recent stress aged them both in ways they would never understand?

She had to remind herself to focus on the issue at hand.

"Babe, what happened?"

Jade abandoned the coffee cup on the counter, almost dropping it, and crossed the chasm of the kitchen to be with her wife. Cass broke into sobs before her head reached Jade's shoulder. Her rash-covered arms hung limp at her side. Jade squeezed her tighter but kept a well-trained ear tuned in the direction of the staircase. All she heard was the high-pitched and constant ringing that fed the throb of her headache.

Cass tried to speak a couple of times, but strangled croaks were all that came out, like she was drowning – choking – on her words. She scratched at her already raw skin, despite Jade's lackluster attempts to dissuade the behaviour. Fresh blood oozed out of old scabs before Cass stopped. She gave up on everything and surrendered to the tears instead.

"It's not fair," she said at last, her own tears brewing. They burned in a way she hadn't expected them to. Like acid. "They're not sure what happened."

There was no laugh from upstairs this time, but Jade shivered all the same.

"She hit her head, but they're still going to do an autop–"

Cass struggled to say the word until bile rose into her throat, and she wrenched herself from Jade's arms. Heaving into the kitchen sink and choking on her own snot and tears. She was only vaguely aware of Jade rubbing her back and telling her that everything was going to be okay. A lie, and they both knew it. It didn't matter. Nothing mattered. Not right now. Maybe not ever.

With Cass crouched on the floor, Jade massaged her wife's hands, scrambling to think of anything else she could do or say that would be remotely helpful. She certainly had never been this close with her own mother. And Vera was – had been – a phenomenal mother and mother-in-law. And an even better grandmother.

"I don't know what to do," Cass whispered.

"I don't know that there's anything we can do. But when the time comes to... to deal with things, I'll be right by your side. The whole time."

Cass nodded. She was numb inside, and her lips barely moved as she spoke. Her eyes focused on nothing.

Jade gripped her wife's hands, squeezing them like they, too, were at risk of breaking, and took a deep breath. But she could not fight back a fresh wave of hot tears. The floodgates were open and there was no stopping the emotional outpouring. The most important and unspoken question between them was enough to shake her resolve. She rested her forehead on Cass's and cried. Keeping an ear out for other sounds within the house was an afterthought. Even the whining in her ears melted out of existence.

"What are we going to do?" moaned Cass.

Jade could think of nothing to say. Her stomach churned as she thought about the inevitable.

"Babe," she managed, "what are we going to tell Willow?"

Cass's voice came out in a whisper. "What if she already knows?"

Jade stared into her wife's eyes with painful intensity. She knew the answer but couldn't make herself say it.

The sound of the floor creaking behind them was like a gunshot echoing through the house. Both women held their breath. The sudden silence that followed was agonizing.

Standing at the entrance to the kitchen was Willow. Her hair was tangled from sleep, but her eyes were bright and alert. A tortoiseshell cat rested in her arms with its head and front paws perched on her shoulder. The little girl absentmindedly stroked the cat's fur while staring at her mothers with the kind of seriousness that suggested she was much older than six. The voice that came from her small mouth might as well have been centuries old.

"Grandma's not coming home, is she?"

Five Months Earlier
September

"Last box!" Cass called out from the living room.

"I'm almost done in here," said Jade, closing the kitchen cupboard. "I don't know what we would do without your mom."

"Yeah," said Cass with a chuckle. "We would never be able to finish all the unpacking if Willow was running around telling us what to do. I'm surprised Mom was able to keep her out this long. I'm going to owe her a drink."

"Well, Willow does love her walks. But I meant... Well..." Jade swept her arms in a circle, motioning to the house. "I think we owe Vera more than a drink for co-signing on the mortgage."

It was two stories, with three bedrooms, two bathrooms; and although the kitchen wasn't huge, this was the most counter space Jade had ever had in her adult life. It was a striking change compared to their two-bedroom, one-bathroom basement apartment that had flooded early in the summer.

After a week at a shabby hotel, their landlord informed them it was safe to return. Jade should have listened to her gut and never let her family back in that place.

It wasn't long before both Jade and Cass noticed that Willow was starting to cough more. Then came the wheezing. They didn't even get a chance to take her to their family doctor. Next thing Jade knew, she and Cass were huddled together in a hospital waiting room while their five-year-old was strapped up to devices Jade didn't even know existed.

Out of both grandmothers, only Vera came to visit. Agnes, as per usual, kept her distance. Vera and Cass had had their problems, but both had been to therapy to resolve any lingering issues. Agnes and Jade, on the other hand, weren't so lucky. Jade had gone to therapy, but her mother refused.

Agnes was a hard woman who couldn't resist the chance to nitpick someone's appearance, weight, lifestyle choices. Even if something was perfect, she could find a way to complain about it. Jade spent most of her adult life fighting not to become the pessimist her mother had been.

Once Willow was released from the hospital, Vera was the one who offered them a place to stay in her own tiny apartment so that they didn't have to go back to a mould-filled basement. Jade had to call Agnes several times to remind her to at least send Willow a get-well-soon card if she didn't want to visit her only grandchild.

She felt no remorse when Agnes was hospitalised less than a month later. She visited as little as possible and only allowed Cass to bring Willow when it was clear that it was time to say their goodbyes. Willow bawled at the funeral as if she had known her estranged grandmother intimately. Jade never even shed a tear.

"Okay," said Jade with a sigh. "I'm done in the kitchen. What's left?"

"Not much," said Cass, kicking an empty box across the floor. "By the way, I can't remember if I told you or not, the cable company is sending someone over tomorrow to set up the TV and internet."

"I'll be home," said Jade with a shrug. "Willow too. I'm thinking we give her at least a week to settle in before sending her back to school. She's already missed the first week, and I don't want to push her."

"Personally, I think we should just send her back now. Might help make things feel more normal."

"Yeah, but she's been dealing with a lot of anxiety these past few months and..."

"Oh," said Cass. "*She's* the one who's dealing with anxiety? Got it."

Jade tossed a wad of packing paper at her wife.

"I'm serious," said Jade, fighting a smile. "I don't want to cause any more damage. I... I want to do what's right for her."

Cass sighed. "I get it. But we've got to let her live. Let her go to school and be a normal kid. Let her make her own bad decisions. And don't think I don't know what this is really about," said Cass when Jade opened her mouth to speak. "You've been a stay-at-home mom for over five years and you're starting to feel the threat of an empty nest looming overhead. Don't deny it."

"I won't."

This time, Cass tossed the ball of packing paper at Jade.

"And I don't want you stuck moping at home. I mean, Mom will be here, but she's got her own life and stuff she does during the day. You need to leave the house too."

"I know, I know," said Jade, busying herself by starting to clear away the paper and boxes. "I've kind of been working on my resume, but I keep putting it off."

"That's good! Hey, and when Willow's at school, you'll finally have some uninterrupted time to finish it. Have you thought any more about where you'll apply?"

"A little. I don't want to disappear. Not like my mom did. I still want to be able to be home for Willow when she's not at school, and it might be fun to volunteer for a few field trips. So, I'm thinking something part-time. Like just an easy café job or whatever. I don't know."

"Ah, I see." Cass stroked an imaginary beard. "You like having me be the sugar mama of the relationship."

Jade laughed.

"It's a good plan," said Cass. "Really."

"Yeah. No matter what, Willow's happiness and well-being come first."

"And no more anxiety," added Cass.

Jade rolled her eyes. "I can't make any promises on that one."

October

Willow's squeals filled the house before Vera and Cass made it through the front door. Her face had been pressed up against the windows of the living room ever since she heard the second-hand sedan rumble up to the driveway. Her tiny face and hands left blurry imprints behind, greasy smears on the window that didn't bother Jade. She was just happy to see that unrestrained joy on Willow's face.

By the time the car doors slammed shut, Willow was already hopping through the house. Thrifted picture frames trembled on the as-of-yet unpainted walls. Even the family pictures taped in place – edges worn and wrinkled from water damage – shook.

"Child, enough," said Cass as she tried to keep a straight face, struggling to make it through the doorway with her oversized bags. In her excitement, Willow was preventing her mother and grandmother from coming in the door.

"She's been insufferable since you two left," said Jade. She placed her hands on Willow's shoulders and guided her out of the way of the doorframe.

Willow said nothing – nothing coherent. Her hopping from foot to foot transformed into spinning while she giggled at the ceiling.

"It's a miracle you survived the day," said Vera as she lowered her share of the shopping bags to the ground. She stood up slowly and both her knees popped. "But now we're here to rescue you!"

Willow rushed at the bags before anyone had a chance to stop her. Each Halloween decoration was removed, examined, and screamed about until she moved onto the next and began the cycle all over again. The child was precise and methodical in her own way, but to the adults this ritual happened at lightning speed.

"This is why Grandma drinks," said Vera, only half joking.

"And *this* is why I didn't want to bring her shopping with us," said Cass, low enough that only her mother could hear.

Vera nodded. She was not one to admit she was wrong, but given the circumstances, she was willing to make an exception just this once.

"Looks like you two had fun," said Jade, eyeing the bags that Willow was rummaging through. Her voice came out more tense than she expected. She clenched her hands into fists within her pockets and forced a smile to her face for the sake of her daughter.

"Don't worry, babe," said Cass, giving her a squeeze on the shoulder. "We stayed under budget."

"Thrift store," said Vera. "They bring in about an aisle's worth of new stuff this time of year. Plastic, but beggars can't be choosers. Plus, there's all the 'previously loved' merchandise. Dirt cheap, and it won't make a difference to the neighbourhood trick-or-treaters."

"So, we can still afford the house," Cass said as she went to kiss her wife on the cheek.

"If we could afford the house, your mother wouldn't be living with us," Jade said, throwing Vera a wink.

Vera howled with laughter. This was enough to distract Willow from her unpacking.

"What's funny, Grandma?"

"Capitalism," she answered dryly.

"Oh," said Willow, as if she understood. Normally, she would pester the adults until she was either in on the joke or she massacred it with her questioning. But today, Willow had other, more pressing priorities. She returned her attention to the haul from the thrift store. A fresh, new squeal filled the house.

"Little Boo, I know you love Halloween, but I think we could do without the screaming right now," said Jade. She couldn't tell if the ringing in her ears was from an oncoming headache or the after effect of the sonic warfare occurring in the front hall.

Willow screamed directly at her mother as if to challenge her. Her mouth was open as wide as possible but the corners of her lips turned up and her eyes sparkled with mischief.

"Well, at least she doesn't get that from our side of the family," Vera said to Cass, elbowing her in the ribs.

"This one goes with Baby Vampire!" shouted Willow as she held up a plastic bat, oblivious to the adults' conversation.

"We don't have Baby Vampire anymore, remember?" said Cass as she crouched to face her daughter. "We had to throw out the old decorations."

"Why?"

"Because they went bad."

"Why?"

"Because of the mould."

"Why?"

"Because of flooding at our last home."

"Why?"

"Because our landlord didn't take care of the building."

"Why?"

"Because Mama said so."

Willow stared into her mother's eyes.

"Why?"

"Because, because, because!" said Cass as she scooped Willow up and tickled her all over. New shrieks ensued and Jade smiled despite the ringing in her ears.

While Cass kept the little girl occupied, Jade swooped in to help her mother-in-law unpack the bags. Willow's attention could only be diverted for so long before she would dive right back in and slow down the whole operation. She would want to help decorate too, so it was best to get the unpacking done quickly at least.

Jade got to work, cutting the price tags and packaging away, peeling off stubborn stickers with her fingernails. Without warning, Willow re-emerged after being chased around the living room. Her little hands were all over the plastic decorations before a winded Cass made it to the fridge for a glass of water.

"Hey, go help your grandma put this up," said Jade as she handed her child a gaudy, tinsel-covered Halloween wreath.

Jade couldn't tell if this was one of the thrifted finds or one of the new, cheap ones. It was hideous, but her daughter didn't care. It was purple and black mixed with a putrid shade of green. Most importantly, it had a frog in a witch's hat on it, so Willow ribbitted and hopped all the way to the open front door, where Vera was waiting.

That particular distraction did not work for long. Once Willow instructed her grandma *exactly* where the wreath was supposed to hang and at what angle, she bounded right back over to her mothers.

"Boo!" she yelled as hard as she could at Cass.

"Indoor voice, please," said Jade to apparently no one as her wife feigned the fright of her life and collapsed to the floor. Willow continued to shout her boos at a pretend-dead Cass.

But Cass, too, was soon ignored when Willow's attention gravitated towards the next new Halloween decoration: a stuffed pumpkin, perfect for squeezing and throwing at parents.

Before handing the inevitable weapon to her child, Jade snuck in a big sniff. There was the faint hint of thrift store, but the overwhelming smell was plastic – blessed new materials.

The next few hours consisted of Jade passing Willow a decoration and telling her where she wanted it to go. Eight times out of ten, Willow would give it a name before bringing it to Cass or Vera, especially if it had anything resembling a face, but sometimes not. Luna-Luna, Silly Zombie, Robo-Man, Mister Kitty, Purple Spider, Stick. The names were endless and nonsensical. Then Mama or Grandma would help her put up the decoration, and Willow would run back to Mommy for the next thrifted treasure.

Jade vetted each item carefully. It's not that she didn't trust her wife and mother-in-law to pick out good decorations. She didn't want to keep anything that would hurt her child. The anxiety did not allow her a moment's rest and came with an accompanying headache.

But she had to do her best to put that all behind her now. It was hard to move on from the recent past, but new decorations for Willow's favourite holiday was a start.

"Mommy's running out of ideas. Where should we put this one, Little Boo?"

When Jade picked up the decoration – a black ram skull – she was surprised by the weight of it. It looked like plastic but felt like bone. She examined it under the light, wondering if her eyes were playing tricks on her. She didn't remember seeing it before now. It was just there in the pile on the counter with the other decorations, like it had been there the whole time. Then again, she'd been at this so long that she could no longer remember which decoration she had pulled out of the bags first.

"What's that?" asked Cass from across the room.

"You tell me. It was in the pile. I don't remember taking a price tag off this one at all." She said that last part to herself.

Cass took a few steps towards her wife, examining the thing closely, but the puzzled expression didn't leave her face. She glanced back at Vera, who claimed she only needed to rest her eyes but was now snoring on the couch. "Maybe Mom grabbed that one."

"There's just something..."

"What?"

Jade shook her head. "Nothing. I'm probably tired too."

"Yeah, it's been a long day." Cass wrapped an arm around her wife's waist and gave it a squeeze. "I mean, maybe I did pick it and forgot. It looks like the kind of witchy stuff you like, so I guess I added it to the cart without thinking about it."

With a shrug, Jade held the decoration out to Willow. It was only in that moment that she realized her daughter was calm and quiet for the first time all day. Willow's tiny eyes widened and her mouth hung open. She ran her fingers over the blackened skull, then pinched the tips of the horns. Jade shivered without knowing why.

"So?" began Jade, startled by the sound of her voice.

"Skull Daddy," Willow whispered.

"What?" said Jade, almost laughing. She couldn't tell if she found the name funny or unsettling.

"Skull Daddy," Willow said a little louder. "That's his name."

Cass sniggered.

Willow whipped her head around and glared at her Mama.

"I didn't say anything. It's an interesting name. Where did you hear it?"

The toddler furrowed her brow. "He's a skull, and he's going to be my new daddy. He told me so himself."

"Ah, okay," said Jade. She always knew the day would come when Willow would start to question the fact that she had two moms and no dad, but she never expected this was the way it would happen.

Cass, however, seemed unbothered by the connotations of the thing's name and was willing to play along. She spoke in a high-pitched, make-believe tone. "Hi, Willow! I'm Skull Daddy. Nice to meet you."

"That's not what he sounds like," Willow said. Her voice was hard, but hushed, like she was afraid the thing would take offense to her mother's mimicry.

Jade shivered again. "So, where will we put him?"

Willow stared deep into the darkened sockets of the skull without blinking. She was an intense child by nature, but there was something unnerving about the way she gazed at the decoration. Something that made the hairs on Jade's body stand on end. She wanted to drop the skull to the floor and let it break so that she wouldn't have to look at it all month.

"He's going in my room," said Willow after a significant amount of time. "He's going to watch over me and keep me safe."

"You sure about that, kiddo?" asked Cass. "Won't that give you nightmares?"

"No."

"Well, she's the boss," said Cass, looking to her wife with a shrug.

Jade was unconvinced.

"I don't know." She looked to Cass for help, and her face crinkled with concern.

"Hey, our kid's done weirder things. Besides, it's just for Halloween. And if she gets spooked or starts having bad dreams, we bring it downstairs."

"All right," said Jade, letting out a sigh. "Just for Halloween. And if you have a nightmare, one single night when you try to crawl into bed with us, Sk..." Jade struggled to get the name past her lips. "Skull Daddy is coming downstairs to the front hall so he can scare the trick-or-treaters instead. Deal?"

"Deal," said Willow with the firmness of an adult in the midst of a serious business decision. In that moment, Jade thought her daughter looked at least a decade older, if not more. Her eyes were dark and focused as she pressed her palms against the top of the skull. Her tiny fingertips explored the uneven surface.

Then, as if changing the channel on the TV, Willow became her usual self again, screaming and running with joy throughout the downstairs of the house. Jade was left holding the skull, feeling sick to her stomach, while Cass went to grab the hammer and nails.

Jade turned it around in her hands, looking deep into the sockets, wondering what her daughter saw in the darkness. She could have sworn it was staring back at her, and was relieved when Cass took the skull away to go hang it up in their daughter's room. Once Cass was upstairs, and Willow's attention flitted back and forth between a pumpkin toy and the hilarity of her snoring grandmother, Jade vomited into the kitchen sink.

November

It took Jade a moment to lock onto the sounds. A low hum of activity that she had to strain to hear clearly. Yet its presence was enough to draw her attention. At first, she couldn't tell if it was coming from the TV or not, but when the light fixture on the ceiling shook, she had her answer.

"I'm going to go check on Willow," she said to Cass, rising from the couch.

"Something up?" Cass didn't turn her attention away from the TV, but she was familiar with that tone of voice.

"I don't know. I would just feel more comfortable if I checked on her."

"She's probably fine," said Cass.

"Right," said Jade, but she made her way upstairs anyway.

With each step, she got closer and closer to the source of the perceived disturbance. Unintelligible words and a thump came from the direction of Willow's room. Something hit her bedroom door and it quivered in its frame.

"Stupid!" came a muffled cry of frustration.

"Willow, what is going on in here?" asked Jade, easing the door open by an inch, poking her head into the room.

"Get out! Close the door!"

"Don't yell at me," she said, although she closed the door behind her as she slid into the room. "What's the matter? Do you want to talk about it?"

"Orange Shark is the worst!" screamed Willow as snot shot out of her nose. Her face and shirt were already soaked with tears.

"Oh, Boo, why? You love Orange Shark."

"He's the *worst*!"

"Inside voice, please. What did Orange Shark do to upset you?"

"He's stupid."

"Willow, please don't use that word. Come on, tell me what's wrong. Let's talk this out."

"He doesn't know how to spell," she wailed.

"He doesn't?" Jade crouched to the floor, leveling herself with Willow's pouting face. "I can see how that would be frustrating."

"He keeps forgetting letters."

"He does? Well, it happens to the best of us. I'm sure he just needs more practice."

But her reassurance wasn't enough. Tears rolled down Willow's cheeks in fat drops.

"He's... stupid."

"Oh, sweetie, Orange Shark is not stupid." Jade wrapped her arms around her daughter and gave her a squeeze. It took only seconds for her shoulder to feel damp. "He has a very good teacher, and the two of you will figure it out together."

"But what if he doesn't? What if he *never* remembers?"

"Give it time, Willow. It's going to be okay. You're– I mean, Orange Shark is still new to kindergarten. It's going to take some time before he learns everything. And that's completely normal. Besides, you– the two of you missed the start of the new school year, so it's only natural that Orange Shark is a little bit behind right now."

Willow uttered a feeble sniffle in response.

"And kindergarten can be scary," continued Jade. "All school can be scary. There's a lot to learn, and you're dealing with changes, and... and even though it gets easier, it's still stressful. It's okay to feel this way and to cry. I struggled in school too. What you're going through is normal."

"Is that why you don't have a job?" asked Willow. She was still whimpering, but there was a touch of uncharacteristic malice in her voice that made Jade's chest tighten.

"I... No, Willow, that's not..." Her tongue was thick and her skin prickled. There was a faint ringing in her ears.

"Boo, I haven't been working because I've been taking care of you, and that's more important. Mama was the one who went to work so I could stay home and be with you while you were a baby. But now that you've started school, and Grandma is here to help out, I've only started applying to jobs. You know that. Just because I didn't do well in school when I was a kid doesn't mean I can't get work. That's not... Is that something you're worried about? Or are you scared that I won't be around as much when I find a job?"

"It's okay, Mommy," said Willow as she wiped her face with the collar of her shirt.

Jade nodded, unsure of what to say next.

"Willow, if you are having a hard time, all you need to do is tell me and Mama. Or Grandma. And the three of us will help you with whatever you're struggling with. Even if it's not a school-related problem. We're a family and we're here for each other. We're here for you. So, it's okay. You're going to be okay."

"Even if I don't know all the words?"

"Especially if you don't know all the words."

"But it's *important*," Willow whined, and the way the whine continued and threatened to turn into a sob told Jade there was an imminent meltdown on the way if she didn't resolve the situation fast.

"Well, sure it's important, but there are lots of other things that are much more important than the alphabet."

The whine stopped in its tracks but lingered in the wings.

"Like what?"

Jade wiped the tears from Willow's face with her own shirt sleeve.

"Like not giving up. Like making friends, being a good person..."

"No!" The whine was back, obscuring the word that burst from Willow's mouth.

Jade composed herself before continuing, and stole a glance at her watch to gauge if either a nap or a snack might serve as a temporary solution to the problem.

"Willow, trust me, this isn't something you need to worry about. It's okay. You don't have to know the entire dictionary right this second. You have plenty of time."

"No, I don't. I have to learn the whole thing by heart fast." Her words were punctuated by sniffles and sighs. There was now a healthy amount of snot oozing from one nostril. Jade wiped her daughter's nose and face.

As Willow squirmed in her grasp, Jade saw how much chalk dust her daughter was covered in. Without batting an eye, she slipped the dirty shirt over Willow's head and replaced it with a clean one before the meltdown monster had a chance to register the change.

"I think it's nap time, Little Boo. We can talk some more about this once you've had a good rest."

Her bottom lip quivered, but Willow nodded reluctantly.

"Besides, while you sleep, your brain goes over everything you learned in the day. It works hard to make sure the information sticks in and stays put. And by the time you wake up, it's all going to be stuck in there like glue."

She grabbed Orange Shark and stuffed him under the covers with her daughter.

"I bet you'll find that Orange Shark has a much easier time remembering all the letters in the words after your nap. I guarantee it."

"It better work, Mommy." An edge of cruelty returned to her voice.

Jade kissed Willow on the forehead, willing to write it off as pre-nap grumpiness, but the continued tightening in her chest warned her it was something more.

"It will. You just have to rest and be patient."

"Cause I gotta know how to spell."

"And someday, you will. You'll be spelling up a storm, writing stories, cookbook recipes, you name it. You're a smart kid."

"But what if I'm not."

"You are. And I believe in you." Jade brushed the hair from Willow's face and waited for sleep to take her. Or for a signal that her presence was no longer required. "Go to sleep, Little Boo. It's nap time."

"Fine. Goodnight, Mommy. Goodnight, Skull Daddy."

With a chill running down her spine, Jade looked up into the dark, hollow eyes of Skull Daddy. The ringing in her ears rose in pitch, drowning out the sounds of Willow's heavy breathing and the sound of her own heartbeat. Her own eyes burned as she gazed into where the ram skull's should have been. And although there was nothing there in those sockets, nothing to keep her frozen in place like this, he was looking back.

December

"How 'bout now?"

Willow didn't look up from her colouring book – the tip of her pencil stayed glued to the page as she scribbled furiously – but she followed Vera's movements out of the corner of her eye, knowing it was only a matter of time before she got what she wanted. Grandma was a strong woman on her own, but grandmothers were known to cave in to the whims of their grandchildren.

"Not yet," said Vera with mock sternness. She knew how this game was played and had years of experience under her belt.

Being a grandmother was decidedly a weakness, but she could be tough when she needed to. She had her ex-husband to thank for that. Nothing could break her. Not even the irresistible smirk of an impish child.

Willow looked up from her drawing and placed the flat end of the colouring pencil on her cheek in contemplation. She glared at the clock she didn't yet know how to read, willing the time to bend in her favour.

"Um, how about now?"

Vera cupped her granddaughter's face in her hands.

"I will tell you when. Would a little patience kill you?"

"Yeah."

Vera sighed. "Last time we went through this, I caved too soon and you burnt your mouth. Well, not today child. Grandma's determined to be the bad guy, no matter the cost."

"Okay."

The pencil never made it back to the paper.

"How about now?"

"Willow, enough," said Vera.

Grandma's "no-nonsense" voice was enough to turn Willow's attention back to her colouring book and away from the cookies cooling on the counter. But her smile still remained.

She beamed when she heard a key turn in the front door. Reinforcements had arrived. But she didn't run up to her mothers right away. Playing the long game was the way to win this particular war. She was prepared to show patience with her parents if it got her a cookie sooner than her grandmother planned.

"We're home!"

After a brief shuffle of winter coats and boots in the narrow entryway, Cass and Jade came in with an armful of groceries each.

"Ooh cookies," said Cass, dumping the bags on the kitchen counter.

"Careful, they're–"

"Ow! Ah!"

While Cass struggled with the cookie, chewing with her mouth open and exhaling the hot air, Vera shot Willow a knowing glance.

"So, I can have one now?" Willow asked.

"No, child. Have you learned nothing? I told you they were too hot, and your mother just burned herself," she said loud enough that her daughter – who was far too occupied with the fresh cookie – would hear her.

"Wait till they cool down," said Jade as she maneuvered around her wife to put the groceries away.

Willow rolled her eyes and returned to her colouring. But although the bulk of her attention was focused on the paper in front of her, she kept stealing glances at the counter where the cookies rested.

"What're you drawing, Little Boo?" asked Cass as she sat next to Willow at the kitchen table, blocking her view of the cookies.

With a simple grunt of accomplishment, Willow twisted the colouring book towards her mother. It was a snowman, covered in the messy scribbles of a five-year-old who made little attempt to colour within the lines.

"That's beautiful. What's all this part here?"

"Dead bugs. To make the snowman stronger. He needs their energy."

"You are one weird kid. She takes after you," she called out to Jade, who was busy putting the groceries away.

"Hey, I wait until you're all asleep before I watch my scary movies. She must've gotten it from someone else."

"Yeah, sure."

Rather than engage with her mothers, Willow let out a gasp as her red pencil clattered to the floor. Nothing else was important anymore. Vera materialized at Willow's side with a plate of warm cookies. The squeals of delight only ceased when the first one made its way into Willow's mouth. In the time it took for Vera to pass the plate around the adults, Willow was ready to accept her second cookie.

"I've got a fun idea," said Vera as she lowered herself into the seat across from Cass, cookie in hand. She slid the colouring book away from Willow and closed it, barely hiding her disgust towards the subject matter of the drawing. "How about we write our letter to Santa?"

"I don't need to," said Willow before shoveling a third cookie into her mouth and reaching out for her colouring book.

"What? Why not?" asked Cass. "You love writing to Santa. And you've been practicing your letters. Don't you want to show him how good you are at writing?"

"I already know what I'm getting," said Willow with enough confidence that no adult would dare challenge her.

"You do?" said Vera, playing along. "Well, what is Santa bringing you this year?"

"I don't think Santa's bringing it," said Willow pensively. "Besides, he's not real."

All three adults paused, and the only sound was Willow's chewing. It was only when she went to reach for another cookie that Cass found she was able to move. She placed her hand over Willow's before shifting it to the plate to pull the cookies away.

"I think you've had enough for now."

"Why? Cause I don't want to write to Santa?"

"No," said Cass. "No, that's not why. It's... Well, I think five cookies is a lot, don't you?"

Willow looked her mother in the eye. "No."

Cass sighed.

"Well, tell me, why don't you believe in Santa anymore?"

"Did one of the other kids at school say something?" added Jade. Her back was stiff and she gripped the edges of the counter.

"No." Willow eyed the cookies. "They all still believe in him cause they're babies."

"That's not a very nice thing to say," said Vera.

Willow shrugged.

"So, why don't you believe in him anymore?" asked Jade.

Willow shrugged again and reached for her colouring book. "I know what I'm getting and Santa's not going to bring it. And if Santa doesn't bring presents like people say, then that means he's not real."

"Okay, now I'm really curious," said Cass. "What *exactly* do you think you're getting for Christmas?"

"A cat."

Cass glanced at Jade, who was now looking at her phone with a furrowed brow. With no backup, Cass took a second to compose herself before entering into what she expected would be a difficult conversation. She wasn't up for breaking her daughter's heart so soon after she realized Santa was nothing but a group of guys who dressed up at the mall.

"Willow, Mommy and I talked to you about this. We really want a cat too, but we're still on the waiting list with the shelter, and it is a long list. There are lots of people who want to bring home a new pet, but it's not kitten season yet, so there aren't as many available. Hopefully, we'll get a cat real soon, but I don't think it's going to be in time for Christmas. It might be sometime in the new year."

"No, I'm getting a cat," Willow said matter-of-factly. "Skull Daddy said so. He's going to bring it to me, not Santa. He promised."

"Jeez, she's still playing with that thing?" muttered Vera.

"Yeah, Willow, don't you think we should put Skull Daddy in the Halloween bin until October?" said Cass. "Wouldn't you like... a sparkly wreath in your room for Christmas instead? One with twinkly lights?"

"No, I like keeping him in my room. He tells me stories and helps me with my schoolwork. He's very nice to me and he gives me things I want. And I want a cat."

Cass sighed. This was one battle she didn't think she could win. Most of all, she worried about the impending meltdown on Christmas day when Willow realized there was no cat. She glanced back at Jade for support. She was still on her phone, eyes darting over the screen and wide with surprise.

"Everything okay, babe?"

"What is it, Mommy?" Willow looked up from her colouring book as if she already knew.

"It's an email from the shelter," Jade said, fighting back a smile, trying her best to draw out the suspense as she joined the others at the kitchen table. "One of the adoptions fell through and we're next on the list."

"What?" said Cass. "You're joking."

"That's... impressive timing," said Vera, stealing a nervous glance at Willow.

Jade turned her phone around to show everyone. There was a picture of a small tortoiseshell cat with big eyes and a shiny coat.

"Her name is listed as Princess, but we can change that."

"Uh, yeah," said Cass. "We don't need a princess in this house."

"She's three years old," continued Jade. "No health issues, no temperament problems; although she needs to be the only cat in a home. Not a problem here. And her foster family says she's great with kids. I'm arranging a meeting with them now so we can meet Princess in person. If we like her, we can sign the adoption papers."

Cass stared at her wife in disbelief, scratching her arm like it was an anxious tic. Vera sat there with her mouth open while Jade beamed.

"I guess we're finally getting a cat! It's a Christmas miracle!"

Willow leapt out of her chair and jumped up and down, screaming with delight. Then, looking Cass square in the eye, she reached for another cookie and bit into it.

January

Hazel – or as Cass jokingly called her, The Artist Formerly Known as Princess – was indeed great with kids, as her foster parents had indicated. Willow was rarely seen without her little mottled shadow and could carry the cat around in any configuration. Upside down, right side up, sideways, folded, pretzelled, Hazel never uttered a peep of discontent. And although she showed the appropriate amount of affection to the three adults in the household, she would leave them in a heartbeat if Willow so much as breathed in her general direction.

This turned out to be a blessing, as Willow was once again struggling in school, and having a furry friend to share her feelings with when she came home was helpful. Although her teacher was concerned about her performance in the classroom, the issue at hand was Willow's relationship with her classmates. She pulled away from the other kids, reading at her desk rather than engaging in playtime. Worst of all, she now hissed at anyone who came close and often found herself in the principal's office.

"Maybe she wasn't ready to go back to school," said Jade one morning over coffee. "I feel awful. She was so excited to go back in the fall. She even talked about seeing her friends."

"I think it's too soon to pull her out," said Cass. "We need to give her more time. Last year was... was a mess. She lost her home. She and her grandmother ended up in the hospital. Not to mention her other, albeit psychotic, grandmother died. Hell, this time last year I almost got laid off, remember?"

Jade nodded but kept her eyes on her coffee cup.

"And we're *still* going through changes. New house, new pet, Mom moved in with us, you're looking for work. She hasn't had time to settle. I think we need to stick to the plan, stick to the routine, and things will calm down eventually."

Jade furrowed her brow. She doubted it would be that easy.

"Hey, at least she isn't hitting or biting like when she was two. And her teacher hasn't threatened to kick her out yet, so that's good news. This is... Well, not normal, but to be expected. And we've survived worse."

Jade forced a smile, despite the threat of an inbound migraine.

Still, she took her wife's advice and tried to be patient. She kept an eye on Willow in the days that followed, looking for signs of... What? Things to worry about? Things that could be fixed? She wasn't sure.

Part of her resented that Cass got to go out to work every day, leaving any household problems behind. Jade was still struggling to find a job. Still getting call after call telling her she didn't have enough experience or that the time off she took to have a baby was too large a gap on her resume. She was stuck at home dealing with the bulk of Willow's outbursts, Hazel's litterbox, Vera's quips about how a child should or should not be raised. Her migraines intensified in frequency and severity.

But this was the life she chose, she reminded herself. She was the one who brought up the subject of kids on the first date, the one who mentioned it so soon after the wedding, the one who set up the IVF appointments. Jade wanted this all her life, despite the ups and downs. No one ever said motherhood would be easy. Luckily, the end of the month came with a chance – an excuse – to help Willow make and maintain friendships.

"Little Boo," asked Jade, "who do you want to have over for your birthday?"

"No one," said Willow as if it was common knowledge.

"No one? You don't want a big party with all your friends and classmates?"

"Hazel's the only one I need." She spoke as if her mother's questions were not only absurd but offensive.

"Alright, then. We'll plan a birthday party for just us and Hazel."

Jade wasn't willing to start a fight about the issue. She loved how close Willow and the cat were, and she wanted to encourage a love of animals, but not if it meant that she didn't want to be around other people. Was Hazel the reason Willow was pulling away from the kids in her class? It at least explained the hissing.

"Relax," said Cass in bed one night after they discussed Willow's obsession. "It's probably a phase." Still, she was scratching the same spots on her arms like she was anxious.

"Besides, Hazel's still so new she's all Willow can think about. Just wait. Once she opens her birthday presents, her focus is going to shift to those. And then she'll want to have some friends over to play with her new toys. I guarantee it."

The scratching continued.

"I hope you're right," said Jade with a sigh. "You said she'd get tired of the whole Skull Daddy thing and she *still* talks about it, and to it, all the time. It's creepy."

"Yeah, I was kind of hoping Hazel was going to help her forget about that. Like it was fine when she was that obsessed with things like Orange Shark or Mrs. Snowball, but with that... *thing* it's different. And I can't put my finger on it."

The scratching grew in intensity.

Jade nodded. "I don't even think she plays with it. She just talks to it. Babe! Your arm! Stop!"

She flung her hands out and grabbed Cass's wrists hard enough to hurt her.

"Ow! What the– Oh. Oh shit. What the hell?"

Cass's arms were bright red streaks of blood and shredded flesh. It was only when she saw the damage that she became aware of the pain.

"I'll grab the first aid kit," said Jade, leaping out of the bed, sparking a mild headache as her ears filled with a shrill ringing.

"I guess I'm more stressed than I thought," said Cass, mostly to herself, as she examined her arms.

The two of them sat in silence while Jade applied ointment and bandages to her wife's arms. When Cass began to speak again, Jade only heard ringing at first until her ears were able to lock on to the sound.

"...time. That's all we can really do for now. And when her birthday comes around, she'll feel more mature, or something. You know how kids are. They like to feel grown up sometimes. And she'll have new toys. Besides, there are worse things a kid could play with than a cheap Halloween decoration."

Jade could acknowledge that she was worrying too much over the issue, but she still felt sick to her stomach at the thought of her daughter's recent behaviour.

"You might be right," said Jade with a sigh, massaging her temples. "But I still feel like we should be doing something about this. I'm... I'm going to call Dr. Basford tomorrow."

"If it makes you feel better," said Cass with a shrug. "But I already know what the doctor's going to say. That it's just a phase, or that she's struggling with all the changes, trying to figure out what's normal after what we went through last year. Blah, blah, blah."

Jade frowned. Part of her knew that Cass was probably right, but the other part of her wasn't willing to give up. She followed through and made the call first thing in the morning. When Willow overheard, she protested, whining that she wasn't sick anymore. But when the day came, she accompanied Jade to the doctor's office without a peep.

Once inside, she put on the perfect show. She spoke about Skull Daddy like he was her favourite decoration and nothing more. Every time Dr. Basford asked her a question, Willow found a way to turn the conversation back to Hazel.

Jade had to force a smile the whole time as she kept her hands balled into fists deep within her pockets. Between Cass's dismissal of any issues whatsoever and Willow's façade of normalcy, Jade began to wonder if she was just imagining things, letting the anxieties of the past year get the better of her.

When Dr. Basford assured her that there was nothing to worry about but offered to put in a referral for a psychologist just in case, Jade wanted to scream at the woman. Instead, she accepted the offer and told the doctor she believed that would be the best course of action given everything that had happened with their family.

Back at home, Jade tried to pretend like everything was okay. Just as she had promised herself months before, she made Willow's happiness her primary focus. And while she played with and cared for her daughter, acting like nothing was out of place, she prayed that the imminent birthday presents would make Willow forget all about that stupid skull so that they could finally rip it off the wall.

Maybe, if Jade was lucky, Skull Daddy would "go missing" after being locked away in a storage bin. Maybe they wouldn't find him in time to put him up for next Halloween.

The weekend after Willow's birthday, while Cass and Vera were out on a grocery run, Willow and Hazel played themselves into a coma. Two tiny bodies passed out on the living room floor, curled up with one another, and surrounded by carnage that suggested extensive world-building in a game of make believe. The new toys had been well received, and Skull Daddy's name had not entered into any conversations.

Jade sat nearby, drinking a cup of tea and reading a book – a rare treat these days. Every so often, she put down her book to take another cute picture of the way Hazel crossed her paws over Willow's chest. She finally felt a glimmer of hope that Skull Daddy would soon be a thing of the past, although the anxiety was ever present.

By the time the tea had run its course, Jade took one more look at the sleeping pair before making her way to the bathroom down the hall. When she got back to the living room, however, Willow and Hazel were gone. Jade listened for sounds of mischief that only a six-year-old could cause. She heard nothing. The silence was worse.

"Willow, where are you?"

She told herself she wasn't worried (yet) but she picked up the pace as she walked through the house. Her heart was already pounding in her chest.

"Willow, answer Mommy please. Where are–? *Willow!*"

The scene in the kitchen made her blood run cold. Willow was balancing on a chair, leaning over the counter. She was reaching for the kitchen knives. Hazel was rubbing her face on the knife block, the way she rubbed up against peoples' legs, purring.

Jade lunged forward and scooped Willow up in one fluid motion. Hazel hissed and scratched at Jade, leaving red lines on the backs of her hands. Jade yelped but kept her attention on Willow. Once her daughter was on the ground, she clamped her hands down on Willow's arms, holding her in place and forcing eye contact.

"What were you thinking? You know you're not supposed to use the kitchen knives unless you're cooking with an adult!"

She realized more than just her voice was trembling. She was shaking her child. Jade tried to steady herself with a deep, uneven breath before speaking again. But she couldn't force the tremors out of her body.

"Honey, you can't scare Mommy like that. Okay? What were you trying to do, anyway?"

"I needed a knife." She shrugged and looked at Hazel, who was now pacing back and forth across the kitchen counter, eyes locked on Jade like she was prey.

"But why? Why do you need one?"

While Willow contemplated her answer, her eyes betrayed her when she glanced upstairs in the direction of her room.

Jade was nauseous.

Please, please, please don't say Skull Daddy.

Willow turned her attention back to her mother. And as if she could read Jade's thoughts in her eyes, Willow smiled and said:

"Because."

That didn't make Jade feel any better, and yet she was thrilled Willow hadn't actually said the words she dreaded. It was easier to pretend that everything was fine that way. Easier to chalk this up as childhood shenanigans gone awry.

Hazel reached out and bopped Jade's head with her paw, making her jump. She gripped her daughter's arms tighter. Willow's brow furrowed.

"I'm sorry I scared you, Mommy." Her voice was too smooth, too calm, not at all like that of a six-year-old. "I promise not to do it again. Hazel and I were only playing. We didn't mean to scare you. Honest."

Jade softened her grip, but the knot in her stomach remained. Her head was pounding and her ears vibrated with pain and sound.

"That's alright, Willow. We all do not-so-smart things sometimes. It's... It's alright. How about we go back to playing in the living room for today?"

"Okay, Mommy."

As they made their way back to the chaos of the living room, Jade replayed all of her conversations with Cass where her wife was certain that Willow's obsession with Skull Daddy would dwindle. She wasn't sure she could trust Cass's optimism.

If this doesn't stop soon, thought Jade as she squeezed her daughter's hand, *we might have to get rid of that skull.*

Willow squeezed back and stopped only when her mother yelped. She had dug her nails into Jade's palm enough to draw blood.

February

"I'm surprised the neighbours haven't called the cops on us," said Jade, massaging her temples.

Between the ringing in her ears and the constant screaming, her migraine might as well have already split her head in two, exposing delicate brain matter to the harsh outside environment. She couldn't tell whether she wanted to pass out or vomit. Stars danced in front of her eyes.

"Give it time," said Cass through clenched teeth as she scratched at her shoulders, holding herself in a sickening hug. "If this doesn't stop soon, the police might have a murder-suicide on their hands."

Cass was grateful her mother wasn't around for this. Vera never reacted well to Willow's tantrums. Or her own daughter's tantrums, for that matter. Cass became familiar with the phrase "Mommy doesn't want to see you right now" by age two. It's not that Vera had been a bad mother; she had been unprepared. Cass was a surprise that her piece-of-shit father encouraged Vera to keep. And yet he had been conveniently absent for most of the child rearing. Work – and the accompanying mistress – was always more important.

Left alone to raise a fussy baby she barely wanted, Vera's initial reaction to every inconvenience was to distance herself from the situation, even if it led to further complications. It wasn't until Cass was well into her elementary school years and her parents were in the midst of an inevitable divorce that she began to experience a loving relationship with her mother.

Thankfully, that, coupled with a few years of therapy, meant Vera was a much better grandmother.

Until recently, at least. Vera was trying, but tired easily. Gave up easily. In fact, she only ever seemed to be her usual vivacious self when her granddaughter wasn't around. Vera spent more time out of the house and then went to bed almost the moment she got in, claiming fatigue was keeping her from spending time with Willow.

Cass wasn't sure if that was true or not. Yes, Vera was getting older and no longer had the same energy reserves she once had. But this was also a continuation of a long-established pattern. Vera was always there for the fun parts of child rearing, never the hard parts.

Cass always made it her mission to treat Willow better than she was treated in those early years. Despite long hours at work, she did not want to be absent, not even during the hard times. But she was still human and could only take so much screaming herself. She would give anything to have this be Jade's problem right now. But from Willow's point of view, Cass was the one who started it.

"Willow, please use your words," Jade pleaded when the screaming still wouldn't stop.

The good cop, good cop routine hadn't worked, and good cop, bad cop was failing. It was about to be nothing but bad cop if the kid didn't settle down soon.

"I think it's time she went to her room to cool off," said Cass. The feet of her chair whined against the kitchen tile as she started to ease away from the table.

"No, we are going to work through this," insisted Jade, but the waver in her voice betrayed her.

Willow stomped over to Jade and screamed as loud as she could, opening her mouth wide like a snake unhinging its jaw, before delivering a firm punch to her mother's stomach.

"That's it!" yelled Cass, unable to contain her rising anger. "You're on time out, Willow. We don't hit."

Time for the bad cop. Cass got up so fast the kitchen chair toppled over. Willow didn't flinch, and Jade was still doubled over, too distracted to prevent what was about to happen. Willow turned on Cass and glowered. Her lips curled in a snarl. She screamed again, exaggerating her posture, curling both hands into fists as if to intimidate her other parent into submission.

Cass stood firm. But it was so hard not to move. The itching and burning deep in the layers of her skin was killing her and she wanted to rip it all off. She wanted to scratch at her muscle and bones until there was nothing left. Whatever she was allergic to – at least, the doctors assumed it was allergies – drove her to the breaking point. But this was not a time to let the discomfort win. She clenched her jaw, refusing to show any signs of weakness in front of her unruly child.

"You can either walk to your time-out corner by yourself, or I can carry you. Your choice."

The threat had no effect on Willow, until Cass took a single, unwavering step forward. Willow's resolve faltered for less than a second, and she quickly glanced back at Jade. But the good cop had recovered and backed away from the situation. Now, she would only watch, arms crossed over her stomach, eyes on the verge of tears. With a howl, Willow stomped her way through the house on her way to the time-out corner.

Dishes clinked inside the kitchen cabinets and Cass heard something rattling upstairs.

All this over Valentine's Day cards. The cheap kind from the dollar store.

After Jade told her and Vera about the knife incident, Cass had been watching her daughter's every move, looking for the slightest suggestion that something was not right. Vera distanced herself from the situation – to no one's surprise – prepared to let the parents take the lead. But not before offering a nugget of advice.

"If you're so worried about how she idolizes that skull, why don't you just take it away and put it in storage until Halloween? Or better yet, throw it out."

But Cass and Jade didn't think they were quite at the point where they needed to start taking away their daughter's toys as punishment. Besides, neither one of them could stomach the thought of touching the thing.

Early in December, when she and Jade finally got around to swapping out the Halloween decorations for the Christmas décor, Cass had attempted to put the skull away with everything else. She waited until Willow was out for a walk with Vera before making her move. But the skull stayed stuck to the wall, despite almost an hour of trying. When her bare hands weren't enough, she tried every tool in the house, breaking a screwdriver in the process. She remembered how much her hands burned afterwards and didn't think her skin could handle additional irritation right now.

There were consequences for the knife incident, though. Willow was always under the watchful eye of an adult and banned from any baking with Mommy for two weeks. But the whole time, Willow showed no signs that anything was wrong. She was the perfect child, and Hazel was the perfect cat, and no one in the house mentioned the name Skull Daddy.

Things were getting back to normal until Willow decided she needed to give dead bugs to her classmates for Valentine's Day.

When Cass came home with a packet of red-and-pink dinosaur-themed valentines – with cheesy sayings like "To a Dino-Mite Valentine" and "Nothing can Tricera-Top You, Valentine" – Willow ran up to her room. She returned with her little hands wrapped around a mason jar, hiding the contents within.

"I have a special present for everyone," she said proudly. "It'll give them good luck!"

"Oh, that's such a great idea," said Cass. "What is it?"

Willow removed the top with glee, bouncing from foot to foot. "Hold out your hands, and close your eyes."

Cass did as she was told. Her skin prickled all over as the mysterious items were sprinkled into her cupped hands.

"Okay, you can open them," said Willow.

Without meaning to, Cass let out a scream when she saw what her daughter had given her.

Cass rushed to the garbage to dump the gruesome handful and then washed off the dried – and sometimes still-twitching – wings and legs, barely listening to her daughter's explanations. Willow explained that she wanted to pretty up the cards by taping dead bugs and spiders to them.

While Willow prattled on about her bug collection, Cass scrubbed and scrubbed until her hands were raw, and her knuckles were cracked and bleeding. Willow was proud of an exceptionally menacing-looking bug she found in the backyard with antennae twice as long as it's spindly legs. Longer than its narrow, black carapace. It was one of the ones that clung to Cass's skin no matter how hard she scrubbed.

"M-Mama! What are you doing?" said Willow when she realized her mother had not been listening to her. "W-why are you throwing them out?"

"Sorry, but I don't want dead bugs all over me," snapped Cass. That's what set off the first wave of the tantrum. It wasn't long before Jade stepped in for damage control.

"Little Boo," said Jade when Willow calmed down somewhat, "I'm sure your friends would appreciate the gift, but bugs don't go on Valentine's Day cards. I'll... help you. I can pick through the garbage can and pull out anything that you want to save. Then, why don't we put them all back in the garden where they belong? Sound good?"

There was one thing about Willow her parents had known about her almost since birth: she didn't like being told no, and she hated being told what to do. Cue the second wave.

And now, Cass was escorting her daughter upstairs to the time-out corner because she was a bad mother for not letting her child glue dead beetles onto shitty paper valentines. As Willow screamed sound enough to make Cass's eardrums shake, she struck her mother repeatedly with one small, balled up fist.

"Hey!" yelled Cass, stopping suddenly on the stairs and whipping her head around to face Willow. "Do you want more than just a time out, young lady? We do not hit in this household. Do you hear me?"

Willow forced out another ear-shattering scream.

Yanking her child by the arm, Cass continued to drag her upstairs.

"Until you can learn to treat people better, Hazel is not sleeping in your room anymore, and that Skull Daddy you love so much is coming off the wall. You can have them back when you apologize to me and Mommy."

"No!"

With more force than Cass expected from a six-year-old, Willow tore herself out of her mother's grasp. Rather than walking to the time-out corner in the hallway, Willow scurried in the opposite direction towards her bedroom.

"Willow! You are on time out. You do not get to play with your toys right now. If you continue to behave like this, I *will* take away more of your privileges."

But Willow only picked up the pace and was at a full run by the time she flung herself onto her bed beside a startled Hazel. She grabbed the cat in her arms and glared at her mother.

"I hate you!"

"Willow!"

"You're not even my real mom, you *bitch*!"

The door slammed in Cass's face.

Stunned, Cass stared at the door for some time before she found she was able to move again. Lifting a hand like she was debating knocking, she wanted to say something to Willow through the door but couldn't find the words. Tears she didn't know she had in her rolled down her cheeks. Cass retreated to Jade in the kitchen. She was dizzy and her skin burned.

"Babe, I..." Jade couldn't finish, but her eyes said it all. She heard the whole thing.

"It's fine," said Cass, wiping away the tears with the back of her hand.

"But we didn't... *I* didn't tell her. You know that, right?"

Cass nodded. They decided early on in Jade's pregnancy that it would be for the best if they never explicitly told Willow which one of her parents had given birth to her. But Cass always knew her daughter would find out about it eventually. How could she not when the kid looked so much like Jade? But she never expected it to be used as a weapon against her.

"Look, it... It's fine. She's... It is what it is." Despite the pain in her skin, she felt numb inside.

"Once she's had a chance to calm down, I'll have a talk with her," said Jade, but she didn't sound determined. She was floundering, unable to fully wrap her mind around her child's behaviour. "For her to say that, and then slam the door on you..."

"But she didn't."

"What?"

"I mean, she didn't slam the door on me," said Cass. "At least, I don't... think so."

"What do you mean? Then what slammed up there?"

"It was the door but... Jade, it closed on its own."

"Babe, you've lost me."

"Willow and Hazel were on her bed when the door closed. There's no way she could have reached, even if she was at the edge of her bed. But she wasn't. She was all the way up against the wall, sitting under... under Skull Daddy."

"So, did she throw something at the door?"

"No. No, she was holding Hazel with both hands. It just slammed shut. By itself."

Jade furrowed her brow and pursed her lips.

"Look, I know how it sounds," said Cass. "And I don't expect you to believe me—"

"I believe you."

"What?"

"Babe, I believe you."

Cass looked up at her wife and saw the fear in her eyes. She was suddenly very cold.

March

It was too quiet.

Vera was downstairs, reading in the living room, and her attention was ripped from the page when she became aware of the lack of ambient noise. An old house like this should at least creak and moan as it settles. A house with a child in it should have an additional accompanying soundtrack. The constant shuffling and giggling above her head for the past hour was normal, but the silence that followed spelled mischief when there was a six-year-old involved. Especially this particular six-year-old.

"Willow? How're you doing up there?"

No answer. Definitely trouble.

"What's she up to now?"

With a groan and a creak in her joints, echoing the sounds of the old house, Vera hoisted herself from the couch. It was only in this moment that she regretted offering to babysit so that Cass and Jade could have some much-needed time together out of the house. She wasn't as young as she once was – a fact she denied – but these past few months had taken their toll. Perhaps the chaos of the previous year was catching up with her. Or maybe it was just as simple as growing old.

Vera was one of those women who came up with a smaller number when asked about her age. She lied, and blushed, and pretended to be Cass's sister, much to her daughter's chagrin. She went out to have fun, flirting with boys who could have been her son. She applied thick makeup to hide any telltale signs of age. She was irked by how little energy she had for activities when playtime with her granddaughter left her aching and short of breath.

Not that there had been a whole lot of playtime lately. Maybe it was because she made an effort to be out of the house during the day, or because Willow saw her grandmother was getting older, but Vera was rarely asked to play games anymore. She felt unwanted and discarded, but at least she didn't have to run up and down the stairs. She could sit and read a book while Willow played by herself with the cat. Most importantly, they could be in separate rooms. Vera loved her granddaughter, but her behaviour these past few months was concerning.

"I love being around her when she's her usual self," she said to Cass the other day, "but I'm real worried about this other side of her that's popped up."

Cass sighed. "Me too, Mom."

"I take it you don't think it's just a phase anymore?"

Cass scratched at her shoulder. "I don't know, Mom."

"And go see the doctor about that rash, will you? It's starting to look worse. Might be infected. I don't think it's allergies."

"*Yes*, Mom. I told you; I'll deal with it once this project is done at work. Between that and the kid... Look, I don't have time for myself right now."

"Well, you need to *make* time."

"It's not that easy. I can't abandon my family responsibilities," said Cass. There was a bite to her words. Vera ignored the implied insult, certain her daughter was overreacting.

"Well, then I'll make time *for* you," she said. "You and Jade plan a night out and I'll stay in and look after my granddaughter."

As Vera made her way up the stairs, the knot in the pit of her stomach tightened with each step. She regretted her decision to babysit more and more the closer she got to the top. She repeated to herself that Willow was probably just exhausted from playtime and was napping. Despite saying it in every possible way, she didn't believe it. Not for a second.

Vera paused in front of the ajar door before knocking. She listened for... well, anything. Sounds of play, sleep talking, pages turning in a book. There was a faint ripping noise that sent chills down her spine. In the near silence, the sound of her own knock startled her.

"W-Willow? Can I come in?"

No answer. Vera felt a wave of fear and exhaustion wash over her and decided she didn't have enough energy to cross the threshold.

"I'm coming in to check on you, okay? *Okay?* Well, if you don't answer, I'm... I'm still coming in."

She wished she hadn't.

The first thing Vera saw was Hazel denning in the white, fluffy entrails of Orange Shark. But Willow's once favourite toy was not the only one in a state of disarray. The floor was littered with the carcasses of dolls, stuffed animals, and everything in between.

The headless body of Princess Unicorn sat in a pile of pages torn out of a colouring book. Her head was at the other end of the room with bite marks in it. They could have been from a cat or a child. Or both. Robot Doctor was missing all his limbs, and Jolly Molly had a pair of safety scissors sticking out of her back. Loose eyeballs peppered the room, severed arms stuck out of drawers, and snippets of doll hair covered every surface of the room like ash and snow.

Yet there was an odd cohesion to the chaos. A pattern to the miscellaneous parts strewn around the room. Like Willow had been playing a game that only she could understand. Rune-like markings covered some of the broken toys in the messy scrawl of a child, and the chemical stench of scented markers filled the air.

Perched on her bed, unbothered by the mess around her, Willow sat under Skull Daddy as she read a picture book. Each time she finished a page, she ripped it out and tossed it to the floor. There was a pile of torn and crumpled pages growing out of the empty carcasses of books.

"Willow! W-what...? Did you do this?"

Willow looked up slowly and smiled. It was not the smile of a child.

"Yes, Grandma."

She turned her attention back to her book and tore out another page.

Vera's legs froze beneath her and she couldn't take a single step towards her granddaughter. Her joints ached, screaming for her to stay put.

"Why?"

Willow closed what was left of the book. She appeared totally innocent in that moment, the way the light of an angler fish looks in the depths of the ocean before the teeth come in to view. A faint sneer formed on her tiny lips.

"I had to, Grandma. Skull Daddy doesn't like them. He'll get me new things to play with. Better things. Out with the old." Her gaze lingered a second too long on her grandmother. "And in with the new, he said."

Vera's mouth hung open as she glanced up at the ram skull on the wall. The dark, hollow pits in its face stared back at her. The room began to swim before her eyes and she worried she would faint.

"I don't understand what would possess you to do this. All your books and toys... And you love Orange Shark. Don't you feel sad that you've done this to him?"

Willow shook her head. Her face was calm, but there was something in her eyes that betrayed disdain for Vera.

"Skull Daddy says Orange Shark was getting in the way. He says–"

"That's it!" Like she had been charged by a defibrillator, Vera jumped into action. "I have had it with this Skull Daddy nonsense. That Halloween decoration does not run this household, young lady. And neither do any other imaginary friends you have involved in this. You can bet I'll be telling your mothers about this when they get home. There *will* be consequences."

Willow looked up at Skull Daddy, nodded as if agreeing with something he said, then turned back to Vera.

"Grandma, they're going to take away my books and toys and ground me for a week, but I think I'll be fine. Skull Daddy says so," she added matter-of-factly.

"And I'll be telling them that I think it's time we found Skull Daddy a new home," said Vera, finding venom in her own voice. She spat the words out, as if she wanted to hurt Willow.

There was a bitter taste on her tongue. She took a few steps forward towards the Halloween decoration.

"Maybe a trip to the city dump will be in order. Out with the old, right?"

But a sudden tightness in her chest stopped her. She gulped and tried to speak but her words lost their power. Her heart beat with strained intensity, like it was fighting to pump blood. Fear wrapped itself around her mind. She felt powerless.

Hazel grumbled from within the bowels of Orange Shark and flexed her paws, unsheathing her sharp little claws. Vera took an involuntary step back from the cat. Her gut clenched and a lump formed in her throat when Willow frowned at her. The way the shadows hit her face made her look decades older. And it made her look dangerous. The child slowly shook her head from side to side.

"Skull Daddy doesn't like it when you say things like that, Grandma."

April

Cass tried to be the one to explain things to Willow. But when she opened her mouth, she couldn't find the words. Instead, she dropped to her knees with a thud and held her daughter close, squishing Hazel between them. The cat wriggled out with a meow that was halfway to becoming a growl when Cass started crying again.

"It's okay, Mama. It's okay."

Willow patted her mother on the back. Her voice lacked any significant emotion, like she was only saying what she knew the adults wanted to hear.

Jade wondered if maybe she was confused. This was too much for a six-year-old to comprehend. This was too much for anyone to cope with. And this was not for her to explain. Cass needed to be the one to tell her. Although every inch of Jade's body was screaming to make her daughter understand, to make her show any emotion at all, she stood firm. The ringing in her ears built to a crescendo and she flinched back from the pain. No one but her noticed.

Cass pulled herself away from Willow. She tried once more to speak, but no sound came out. More tears spilled down her cheeks as she nodded for Jade to continue.

"Willow," began Jade again, voice trembling and uncertain. "Grandma had an accident on the way home from the store."

"I know. I told Grandma I needed more pipe cleaners. She was more than happy to leave me."

Jade choked down the rising bile in her throat. "Willow, your grandmother... Well, we don't know exactly what happened yet, but the police found her car and..."

"Grandma's not coming home," said Willow.

That was the second time she said that and it was infuriating. Cass knew how Willow came by that information, but her brain didn't want to admit it. She felt nauseous when she realised the words were surfacing on her lips.

"What do you mean you know, Little Boo?"

Willow pulled away from Cass and shifted from one foot to the other. Hazel circled around the trio and rubbed her body against the back of Willow's legs.

"Did Grandma tell you something?" asked Jade, equally unprepared to face the inevitable truth of the situation. "Was she unwell? Did she know she shouldn't be driving?"

Willow shook her head.

"Please, tell Mommy what you mean," said Jade. "This is important. Did Grandma say something to you before she left?"

"No." She fidgeted with the hem of her dress. "Um, well, she told me she loved me, but it didn't sound like she meant it."

"How can you say that?" moaned Cass. "Willow, she adored you. She would have done anything for you. You understand that, right?"

Willow nodded, but there was no real understanding in her face, as if love was an unfamiliar concept. Jade could tell there was something else her daughter hadn't shared with them yet. Something beneath the surface.

"Willow," Jade began, muscles tense and bracing for the worst. "How did you know that Grandma would not be coming home?"

Willow pursed her lips before looking Jade in the eye.

"Skull Daddy told me."

Cass grabbed Willow roughly by the shoulders and shook her.

"This isn't a game!" she yelled.

The sudden noise was enough to shake Jade out of her macabre reverie, but the headache and nausea remained.

"Cass," Jade muttered as she gripped the edge of the kitchen counter to keep from falling back. No one heard her. Especially not over her wife's frantic shouting.

"Grandma is gone and she is never coming home! Ever! She's dead! Dead! Do you understand, Willow? *Do you fucking understand?*"

"Cass! Stop!"

Cass froze, then released Willow, pulling her hands back as if they burned. She rubbed them back and forth across the rashes on her arms as if that would take away the burns and blisters. Cass didn't realize they were there until the friction from skin-on-skin revealed their existence. She stared at her hands like they were alien objects. With one blink, the blisters multiplied, covering every inch of her hands. With another blink, they were gone and her hands were free from blemishes. She looked up at Jade with fear in her eyes.

Jade sank to the floor, level with the rest of her family. She wanted to throw up but started crying instead.

For the first time, as if it finally occurred to her what was happening, Willow's face wrinkled with emotion. The tears came.

Within seconds, both Willow and Cass were wailing. Jade's feeble tears were nothing by comparison. Hazel pawed at Willow's hand to comfort her, but she paid no attention to the cat. She dove into her mother, and Cass held her tight. Jade crawled forward and wrapped her arms around the two of them. All three bodies trembled as Hazel paced in circles.

"I'm sorry, Mama. I'm so, so sorry," Willow moaned into Cass's shoulder. "I didn't mean to send her away. I didn't mean it. I'm sorry."

May

"Grandma was a filthy whore! Grandma was a filthy whore! Grandma was a filthy whore!"

Willow skipped around the kitchen, with Hazel trotting dutifully behind her, as she chanted the phrase at the top of her lungs. Assorted vases and mugs trembled on countertops and shelves, threatening to spill their contents of half-dead flowers.

Despite any evidence to the contrary, Vera was not the kind of woman who wanted a big funeral. She lived loud but had asked to die quietly. Cass thought that would be best given the circumstances surrounding her death, and Jade supported her decision. Vera was cremated without any ceremony, and her family scattered the ashes in a nearby river. A calm place with a breathtaking view. Friends sent sympathy cards and flowers in droves.

Many of the bouquets contained plants that were toxic to cats. A malicious part of Cass wanted to keep them in the house in the hopes that Hazel would try to eat them, as cats are likely to do. That part of her blamed Willow for what happened and needed her to experience earth-shattering grief and loss.

"Absolutely not," said Jade after Cass gave voice to that particular thought. "We are not putting our daughter through another funeral. Not now." Her words were hard, and she surprised herself with their ferocity.

"It was just a joke," grumbled Cass.

"Was it? She may not be mourning in the way you want her to, but she is grieving this loss in her own way."

"Please, she's just upset because we still won't buy her any new toys after she trashed everything."

"Have you heard her crying in her room at night? Calling out for her grandma in her sleep? Because I have."

"I..."

Jade took a step closer to her wife and brought her voice low to a whisper. "I think we both know that you don't actually blame your own daughter for this."

Without thinking, Cass raised her eyes to the direction of Willow's bedroom.

A couple minutes later, Cass disposed of the lilies, carnations, and baby's breath, taking out the trash afterwards. Everything else was left to die unceremoniously in a thrifted vase or coffee-stained mug.

"Grandma was a filthy whore! Grandma was a filthy whore! *Avia erat meretrix turpis! Avia sordida erat meretrix! Mater tua gallum sugit in inferno!*"

Willow's perverse chant devolved into deep, guttural noises that bore only a passing resemblance to speech. Ceramic shattered on the floor, causing Jade to yelp. Cass stood frozen over what was left of her coffee mug.

"No. No!" said Jade, after her own momentary paralysis had worn off. "We don't talk like that." She looked quickly back and forth between her wife and daughter. "Willow, let's apologize to Mama. Please."

"Grandma was a filthy whore!" Her words returned, but her voice was deeper.

"Willow stop. *Stop!*"

Willow stamped both feet down and squatted facing Jade as she channelled all of her energy into the mightiest bellow she could muster.

"Grandma was a filthy whore!"

The whole house shook, but it was as if it happened in a dream. There was no sound of any furniture being disturbed, no groans from the old house. It wasn't until Willow punctuated her words with a heavy jump, putting all of what little weight she had into the motion, that Jade was aware of an actual, physical tremor in the floor. Vases tipped over, spilling flowers and brackish water all over the kitchen and living room floors.

Before Jade could blink, Cass stepped over the broken mug at her feet and yanked Willow out of the kitchen. Willow started screaming, but Cass didn't flinch. Miraculously, neither did the house or the remaining vases. She kept dragging Willow towards the stairs. As if she were walking through gelatin, Jade forced herself up from the table to follow them. She didn't want to, but she was compelled to all the same.

Willow made her body go limp, dangling at the end of her arm, screaming her head off. But that didn't slow Cass down. She scooped up her daughter, not bothering to do it gently, and carried her up the stairs.

The screaming set off a fresh migraine right behind Jade's eyes. Through blurred vision, she watched as Cass dragged their child higher and higher up the stairs – Jade never realised the staircase was so tall. Her wife's skin was splotchy red and weeping yellow pus. That didn't stop her from lifting a thrashing Willow up above her head and throwing her to the ground below.

Willow's tiny body landed with a small thump, yet the explosion it caused was horrendous. Less than a second after landing, Willow's body exploded into a fountain of blood, splattering Jade with slimy bits of innards. She gagged as a piece of flesh flew into her open mouth. Her skin was greasy and slick with what remained of her child.

Jade watched as her wife's skin sloughed off, almost in slow motion. Cass tripped on the pile of viscera and clothing at her feet, and her bloody body stumbled down the stairs, arms outstretched towards her wife. Jade screamed, putting every ounce of her energy into the act, but no sound came out.

Squeezing her eyes shut until it hurt, Jade fought to clear the illusion from her mind. She prayed it was just an illusion. Gritting her teeth, she forced herself to open her eyes.

The walls were clean and free of blood. Willow was still screaming in Cass's rash-covered but otherwise unharmed arms. Jade spat into her hand, trying to clear the imagined blood and flesh from her mouth, but her saliva was transparent and bloodless. Heart in her throat, she ran up the stairs to catch up, worried something horrific could still happen.

When Cass neared the time-out spot beside the bathroom, Willow's screams were so shrill that Jade thought all of their eardrums would burst. Her head vibrated as if her own bloody explosion was imminent. There was a thud as Willow was roughly deposited into the corner. She was screaming too much to bother crying, although a few stray tears started to leak out of the corners of her eyes.

"What is wrong with you?" said Cass over the incessant screaming. "Why would you say something like that?"

Jade placed a hand on Cass's shoulder in an attempt to defuse the situation, but her hand was shrugged off.

"Willow, can you tell us who taught you that bad word?" Jade's voice was trembling. She wasn't confident she'd be able to keep her cool or keep Cass calm. And she did not want to know where her child learned Latin, or that other, guttural language.

"I just heard it!" yelled Willow.

"Where?" asked Jade, trying to sound a little firmer but knowing she was outgunned.

Willow only scowled before running right into Cass as she tried to escape the time-out corner. Cass was only jostled slightly by the tackle, although she was surprised by the amount of strength her daughter put into it. Still, she was able to manoeuvre Willow back into the corner.

"You are on time out," said Cass.

"Why?"

"Because you can't say things like that about Grandma! Or anyone else. But especially about Grandma."

Jade placed a hand on Cass's shoulder again, and it was permitted to stay. She was grateful. Jade wasn't sure if she was trying to calm Cass so much as she was trying to calm herself. She wanted to run away screaming, tearing her hair out as she went.

"Willow," Jade tried again. "Do you know what it is that you're saying? Do you understand what it means?"

The toughness left Willow's body but remained in her face. There was uncertainty in her eyes and she was now grasping at the hem of her dress.

"Willow?" prodded Jade. Her voice lacked any strength and was now no more than a whisper. "Do you know what that word means?"

"No." For the first time in ages, Willow sounded small. She sounded like a child again.

Jade exhaled slowly, and she felt Cass relax a little under her hand.

"Okay. Can you tell us where you heard it?" asked Jade. "We promise we won't get mad."

A part of her still prayed that Willow picked up those words from the playground at school. This delusional part of her mind was all too eager to forget that Willow had not gone back to school since Vera's death.

Willow's eyes hit the floor and the wringing of her dress became more pronounced. A chirrup from Hazel across the hall brought some of that self-assuredness back into her face as she looked up at her mothers.

"I heard Grandma went to a fair and had a bortion when Mama was little. It's 'cause she was mad at Grandpa and didn't love him anymore. She didn't even love *you*." Her eyes shot daggers into Cass. "And that means Grandma was a filthy whore."

Jade looked at Cass, but her wife was silent and trembling. All of the tension returned to her body and it looked as if the rash was spreading. Jade returned her attention to Willow and dreaded the next question. They'd been asking too many similar questions these past few months, and the answer was always the same. Wasn't that the definition of insanity?

"Willow, who told you this? Who said these mean things about Grandma?"

The squirming stopped, and Willow looked her mother right in the eye. Her gaze never wavered.

"Skull Daddy."

It was over before anyone registered that it happened. The snap of flesh against flesh rang out through the house. Cass was panting with rage but frozen in place after the sudden movement. Willow's cheek turned bright pink before she realized she had been hit. But she didn't cry. She screamed.

Screaming with such force that Jade wondered if the windows were going to break – she thought she saw them quiver in their frames – Willow dashed out of the time-out corner and into her room, pushing Cass so hard she fell over. Hazel slipped into the bedroom and the door slammed shut of its own accord. But still Willow did not cry. The silence that followed was much more unbearable.

"We need to get rid of that thing," said Jade, suddenly wracked with tremors so violent it hurt. Lights flashed in front of her eyes, bringing on a fresh headache that drove her to her knees. "We can't go on like this."

June

Jade's hand slipped and she grazed her fingers with the edge of the knife. She set it down on the cutting board beside the slightly mangled apples she was attempting to slice. Examining her fingers for signs of injury, dark red droplets materialized along the side of her index. But after one heavy-lidded blink, the blood was gone. The only pain she felt was the dull headache that never seemed to leave. She couldn't remember the last time she woke up without a ringing in her ears and a pounding head.

"I need a nap," she muttered to herself.

Instead, Jade went about making her sixth cup of coffee for the day. Or was it her seventh?

"You want any?" she called out unenthusiastically. But she didn't receive an answer. Not that she was expecting one.

Things hadn't been the same since... Well, since they lost Vera. No, that wasn't right. Things hadn't been the same since the arrival of... Jade didn't even want to think it. The words made her tongue and her brain ache.

And then there was the incident last month. There had been a noticeable change after Cass struck Willow. None of them had spoken about it, but the weight of it hung in the air.

Cass was back at work after an extended bereavement period, but she was taking more and more sick days than usual. When she was home, she kept her distance from Willow and Hazel. She even kept her distance from Jade. Cass sat balled up on the couch and tried to ignore the rest of the world, sometimes burying herself in too many blankets in order to achieve the desired effect.

But at least she was able to go into the office about once or twice a week. Although she wasn't sure when – all the days and weeks blurred together now – Jade gave up trying to find work. She stopped getting rejections and now just wasn't hearing back from the companies she applied to. She wanted to believe that that was simply the state of the job market, but deep down she knew Willow had something to do with it. Her daughter didn't want her to leave – especially now that she refused to interact with Cass – so that thing on the wall turned Jade into a prisoner.

She envied Cass's apparent freedom.

Jade was trapped in the realm of stay-at-home mom. She still couldn't talk to Willow about going back to school. And it wasn't that Willow was depressed and struggling with the loss of her last remaining grandparent. Quite the opposite. Willow was thriving and was in better spirits than ever before. But not in the way she should have been.

Jade lacked the mental alertness to describe what she was witnessing in her child, but Willow was too happy. The absence of her grandmother no longer affected her, as if Vera never existed in the first place. The depression and unexplained sluggishness of her parents did not upset or concern her but did aggravate her when it meant snack time was delayed. Willow might as well have been living in her own world, where the problems of adults – and the adults themselves – had no power.

After too many one-sided fights, too many hallucinations of grave injuries, Jade decided it wasn't worth it trying to force Willow back to school. She would go back when she was ready.

If that day ever came. Besides, the school year was almost over, and the principal had been lenient concerning Willow's absences in light of their recent loss. Jade offered to touch base with the school in September when the new school year started. It was still months away, but she already knew that she'd be telling the principal all the same stories and excuses as before.

Coffee in hand, Jade wandered over to the couch and sat beside her wife. Cass stared at the blank TV. Her knees were tucked in all the way to her chin and she was draped in fleece blankets that were usually locked away in the linen cupboard until the colder months. She shivered beneath them as she scratched at the raw, red skin of her arms, legs, and face. She didn't acknowledge Jade when she sat down.

Jade wanted to reach out and touch her wife. Hold her. Comfort her. But she was too exhausted to do so. That's what she told herself, at least. Deep down, she was scared. Cass's moods had been unpredictable ever since Vera's passing. And she wasn't sure if Willow would allow her to socialize with "the bad parent" until the slap was forgotten. If that ever happened.

The coffee warmed Jade's fingers but remained untouched. She was so drained that she couldn't fathom raising the mug those few inches to her lips. It was too much effort. The scent that accompanied the dull warmth was enough for now.

After countless moments of silence, Jade attempted a sip. Her stomach churned in protest. Looking into the murky darkness of the mug, she saw worms writhing around in the hot liquid. Her heart fluttered and she clamped her eyes shut. She was all too familiar with how this game was played. When she opened her eyes, the coffee was free from slimy intruders.

But she wasn't in the mood to drink it. She got up and brought her coffee into the kitchen. She would have dumped it down the sink but got lost in thought and set the mug down on the counter instead, close to the edge.

Jade absentmindedly placed the apple slices on a plastic plate. It was red and white and covered with cartoon ladybugs. It used to be Willow's favourite plate. Just like Orange Shark used to be her favourite toy, and noodles in butter used to be her favourite food. Now, Jade didn't know what Willow's favourite anything was. Hazel and Skull Daddy were the only things her daughter cared about anymore, the only ones she talked to.

She climbed the stairs slowly, listening for the sounds of play and hearing only muffled mutterings. It was unclear whether the words were in English or some other, older language. Her heart leapt with each errant creak in the old floorboards. Jade coughed blood every time her heartbeat increased. Her tongue was thick and heavy with it. But when she wiped her mouth or spit into her hand, there was nothing there. Another illusion.

Jade placed the smallest piece of apple on her tongue to try to clear the gruesome sensation. She spat the masticated fruit into her hand, gagging as she did so, when the familiar sweetness was replaced by pus. A lot of her meals had similar outcomes nowadays.

A few weeks ago, she had tried reaching out to the psychologist. She had completely forgotten about the referral request until she listened to the voicemail. Although she wasn't entirely confident it would resolve anything, she set up a phone consultation anyway.

Unsurprisingly, it didn't help and it didn't banish Jade's sleepless nights. Dr. Hiebert insisted it was perfectly normal for a child to have an imaginary friend. It was normal for Willow to retreat inward after the loss of a family member. Even Jade's insomnia and resulting hallucinations were normal given the circumstances. All she needed to do was take over-the-counter sleeping pills and a good night's sleep would have her feeling like her usual self in no time. Did Jade want to book an in-person appointment at the end of the consultation? No. No, thank you.

At the end of that phone call, she charged up the stairs to Willow's bedroom, not even stopping to think if her daughter was in there or not. She was bursting with desperation and needed to do something. Jade had planned on yanking that skull right off the wall, no matter what it took. But the moment she crossed the threshold, her mind emptied. She forgot why she had entered her daughter's room in the first place.

After standing around for a moment, lost and cringing under the eyeless stare of the thing on the wall, she gave herself a reason to be there by collecting whatever dirty dishes she could find before making a hasty retreat. She didn't remember her plan to remove Skull Daddy until hours later.

Now, standing outside of Willow's bedroom, fresh snack in hand, she shivered. The whispered words coming from the other side of the door made her nauseous, even though she still could not understand them. She wondered if she would ever get a chance to even try prying Skull Daddy off the wall.

"Willow?"

Jade knocked on the door to her daughter's bedroom and the muttering stopped. The silence sucked the remaining life out of the house. The pain behind Jade's eyes and between her ears spiked.

"Willow... I-I've got your snack."

A muffled creak of a floorboard from the other side of the closed door indicated that Jade managed to pique her child's interest.

"I'm coming in, o-okay?"

There was no answer, but Jade was not prepared to wait in that unbearable silence. The sooner she could retreat downstairs the better. She opened the door and braced herself.

"I've got some apple slices for you," said Jade weakly. She stood in the doorway, but her body would not allow her to move any further.

"Oh, thank you, Mommy. Thank you."

Willow abandoned Hazel on the floor and ran to hug her mother's legs. Jade could have jumped out of her own skin. She told herself that she wasn't really afraid of her own child. It was all in her mind. But that was far from the truth. Her fear of Willow was palpable, and her legs burned where her daughter's flesh touched hers. She tried to conceal the sudden urge to gag. Thanks to her association with that *thing*, the mere thought of touching Willow was agony.

Willow took the plate from her mother's hands before running back to her spot on the floor to munch on the apple slices. Usually such a dainty eater, Willow grabbed a handful of apple and violently pressed it to her open mouth. Her teeth clamped down on most of the snack, but not all. The flesh of the fruit tumbled onto her dress while smaller fragments clung to the area around her lips. It looked like maggots, squirming under the light. Jade wanted to vomit.

Hazel rubbed her dark, mottled face against a large mixing bowl from the kitchen that sat between them. It was filled with crumpled bits of paper, twigs, leaves, and dead worms. Something moved underneath the mass of detritus.

"Willow, I'm going to go have a nap. I'm... I'm tired today. Mama's downstairs if you need her. But she's... Be gentle with her, okay? She's still having a hard time."

"Okay, Mommy. You go nap. I'll be fine. Oh, wait! Mommy, before you go, you *have* to kiss Skull Daddy."

Jade froze and her stomach churned worse than it had when she tried to drink her coffee. The acid within her burned as a chill crept into her muscles. Lights flashed in front of her eyes and she gripped the doorway, worried she would faint.

"N-not right now. Mommy's tired."

"Please, Mommy. Please. You'll sleep better if you do. Skull Daddy will make sure you have good dreams. Won't you, Skull Daddy?"

Willow and Hazel turned to look at the thing on the wall, and Jade followed their gaze. It no longer looked like it was made of plastic. And those empty eye sockets stared at her from the wall, daring her to make a move. Jade seriously doubted that the skull had anything good to offer her.

"Willow, I..."

But Willow got up off the floor and took her mother's hand before she could protest any further. Jade's feet led her across the room but she was too tired to fight it. Unable to tear her eyes away from the grotesque thing that sat above her child's bed, she leaned in for a kiss, even as her body screamed at her not to.

She pressed her lips against the skull and determined once and for all that it was not plastic. It wasn't foam, or plaster, or any other kind of material from the Halloween aisle of the thrift store. It was real. Bone. Devoid of all traces of flesh, yet there was a musk of decay seeping out from all of the cracks and crevices.

What was even more nauseating for Jade was that the skull was warm. Too warm for something that was supposed to be dead.

July

Of all the days for the air conditioner to break, this was the worst. It was too hot out to open the windows for a breeze that didn't exist, and the current heat wave meant they were going to have to wait longer than usual for a repair person to come by. The rough estimate the company gave Cass over the phone was that someone would show up by the end of the week. Given their recent luck, Cass would have been surprised if anyone came that soon.

While Cass waited on hold for the second time during that call, Jade ran around the house closing curtains and setting up fans in an attempt to cool the place down. By the time Cass got off the phone, they were both drenched in sweat.

"Why don't we go to the mall or something?" said Jade between gulps of ice water. "Somewhere with AC."

"It's a good idea." Cass glanced upstairs and clenched her hands into fists. "But only if we can get Willow to leave the house."

"That's doubtful," said Jade.

Jade was stumbling through life. Restless nights left her feeling foggy during the day. It was easier to put herself on autopilot and go through the motions of daily life. She took care of Cass, Willow, and Hazel, not because she wanted to but because it felt normal. If she could ensure the needs of the other bodies in the house were being met, it would be easier to ignore her own. If she stopped to think, to rest, the gruesome hallucinations would start.

Although things had improved at home somewhat with Cass back at work full-time in a remote capacity and on speaking terms with Willow again, Willow was still a problem. She went outside to the backyard, at least, mostly in the evening when the summer sun wasn't as harsh, but she did not like to leave the house. The tantrums that erupted from the mere suggestion of family outings were downright horrifying. She didn't dare bring up the idea of going back to school in the fall.

Willow said she couldn't bear to leave Hazel. Although that was true, Jade and Cass knew it was more likely that Willow couldn't bear to leave Skull Daddy.

The only time she willingly let her parents take her farther than the backyard was when she went for a biweekly walk through the neighbourhood. She would lead the way with a fatigued parent stumbling behind her. She didn't want to go to the park or spend time with other children. She didn't want to visit any of the local shops or walk on any of the main streets. She wanted to comb green spaces and empty parking lots for things she could not find in her own backyard. Things she claimed she needed for vague reasons, games of make believe.

Her parents knew who really needed those leaves, and sticks, and bugs, and trash. They were too exhausted, too beaten down to fight it. Willow brought whatever she wanted into their home.

On one of those days Willow informed Jade that it was time for a walk, Cass snuck into her daughter's room with the intention of tearing down that hideous *thing*. It wouldn't budge, no matter how much she tried. It should have been only a simple nail hooked under the lip of the skull keeping it there. And she must have pulled a muscle or strained too hard because her hands ached for almost a week afterwards, like she was bruised down to the bone. The burning rash on her fingers worsened and began to weep yellowish fluid. Cass wore therapeutic gloves every day now.

"We could bribe her," said Jade after a moment of contemplation.

"With what?"

"Anything?" Jade didn't know what Willow liked enough to be used as a bribe anymore. It was easy to talk her into bugs, and plants, and things that could be found outside. She could think of nothing that Willow could want from a shopping mall. Her child was changing beyond recognition.

Cass sighed. "Sure, let's give it a try. What do we have to lose at this point?"

The two of them lurched up the stairs, weary from the heat and the stress. The air was thick at the top of the house, and it was hot enough that Willow had her bedroom door open. The lights were off, Hazel lay panting underneath the bed, and a nude Willow sprawled out beside her on the floor reading a book on insects that had likely been stolen from the school library months before anyone noticed.

A minute glance between her two parents was all the communication they needed to establish a game plan. Jade took the lead as the bearer of bad news.

"Willow, we're going to go out somewhere where they've got working air conditioning. That way we can take a break from this heat. Can you please get ready to go?"

"No, I'm good." She didn't look up from her book.

"We're going to bring Hazel downstairs where it's cooler, and then the three of us are going out. We need to cool down, and so does Hazel. She shouldn't be cooped up in your room."

"She's happy here."

"How's this?" said Cass now that it was her turn to try. "How about we go to the mall and we buy you something? Anything you want. How does that sound?"

Willow half glanced behind her, as if she was looking for Skull Daddy's approval. She turned her attention back to Cass, studying her to determine her seriousness.

"Okay. We can go."

"Easier than I expected," muttered Cass, her shoulders releasing their pent-up stress.

Jade, however, remained tense. This whole situation struck her as too easy. There was no tantrum, no gory hallucination, no headache. Nothing to prevent them from leaving the house. Willow got dressed without another word and carried Hazel downstairs into the kitchen. She placed the cat on the tile floor and brought her water dish within reach. Then she announced that it was time to go.

The day at the mall was equally painless and tantrum-free. To Jade and Cass, none of it felt real. In those moments when Willow got ice cream smeared all over her face or climbed over the beds in the department store, Skull Daddy was nothing but a bad dream. They were a normal family again.

But the bribe was not forgotten. After eating dinner in the food court, Willow informed her parents that they had to go back to The Dress-Up Store as she called it. She told them exactly what she wanted them to buy for her, and she clutched the shopping bag to her chest the whole way home. The only time Willow released it from her grasp was when Jade offered to remove the packaging.

"Gimme, gimme, gimme!" said Willow as she bounced around the kitchen on the tips of her toes.

"What do we say?" said Cass. She never would have given her daughter that instruction had they not returned to some semblance of normalcy. When Skull Daddy was in control, she was too afraid to discipline her own child.

Jade was busy cutting open the plastic packaging of the sparkly fairy wand. It was covered in purple-and-orange streamers and had a shiny purple star on top that flashed orange in the light. It was a normal toy for a normal child. She said a silent prayer to herself that this would soon replace her twisted obsession with the thing in her room.

"Please, *please*."

"Alright, here you go," said Jade, and she felt a genuine smile rise to her lips. "All stickers and tags are gone."

"Yay!"

The noise woke Hazel, and she slinked out from underneath the living room couch to join them in the kitchen. She mustered up enough energy to follow Willow at an elegant trot as she ran through the house, waving her new wand.

Cass sighed and allowed a smile to her face too. "Hopefully all this excitement will help knock her out for the night."

Jade nodded. "Today was good. Normal."

Cass turned to look her in the eye but said nothing right away. "It was. Maybe... things are going to be okay. Maybe it was just a phase. And everything's been so hard for all of us for so long... We probably made it all worse by making it too big a deal. We don't know what normal is anymore, so it's easy to focus on the worst of every situation."

Jade shrugged and she felt a faint pulse of pain behind her eyes. This moment of normalcy might as well have been a dream, yet Jade wasn't willing to relinquish that one shred of hope.

"I would love for all of this to have been nothing more than a bad dream."

"I put a hex on you!" shouted Willow from the entryway, streamers dancing in the air.

"Here we go," said Jade, on the verge of a laugh for the first time in months. She turned to her wife. "Got enough energy left to play along?"

"Hey, if she hexes me so I get to 'fall' to the ground and have a nap, I will play along."

"I put a hex on you!" came the refrain, and streamers fluttered in its wake.

"Uh-oh, sounds like we've got a witch living with us," called Jade in mock fear. "I hope she doesn't get us."

Willow's head popped around the corner with a grin plastered onto her face. She held the wand at the ready.

"Mommy, I put a hex on *you*!"

Cass jumped when Jade screamed, but stopped laughing when she realized her wife's cry had not been pretend. Willow, however, kept giggling.

"Babe, what's wrong? You okay?"

Jade looked down at her legs with one hand over her racing heart. Lines of blood formed on one calf.

"I think Hazel scratched me."

"Shit. Well, she sure picked a good time." Cass chuckled as she went to get first aid supplies from the downstairs bathroom.

"Mama?"

"Just a sec, Willow. I've got to take care of Mommy first."

"Mama, I put a hex on *you*."

The light above Cass's head shattered with a crackle of electricity. Pieces of glass from both the bulb and the fixture fell around her. She managed to raise her hands for protection, at least, but was not fast enough to move out of the way.

Willow cackled wildly as Cass brought her hands down, examining the wreckage that surrounded her.

"Hex, hex, hex, hex, hex," chanted Willow in a singsong voice as she skipped across the main floor.

Hazel stayed behind to watch over Jade and Cass. She sat up on the kitchen counter and looked at the humans, boring into them with her deep-amber eyes. Her tail flicked back and forth.

"What the hell just happened?" asked Cass, not daring to speak above a whisper.

Jade stared at her, lips trembling. She inched away from Hazel, worried the cat might lash out at her again.

"Hex!" came the cry from the living room before the TV turned on by itself.

"Hex!" One of the fans erupted into sparks, spewing smoke.

"Hex!" All the kitchen cabinets opened with a crash.

"Hex!" The cutlery jumped out of the drawer and rained onto the floor.

"Hex!" Water came gushing out of both the bathroom and kitchen faucets, and no amount of fussing with the taps would make it stop.

"Hex!" With a pop, all the lights in the house went dark, the remaining fans stopped, and tendrils of smoke crept out from the front hall closet where the fuse box was.

Cass and Jade could do nothing but stare at one another. But it was not disbelief in their eyes. It was fear.

August

The plastic wand was hidden after less than a day of use. After a few more burst lightbulbs, broken appliances, and shattered windows, Jade and Cass snuck into Willow's room while she was sleeping to retrieve it. Hazel watched with one eye open from the foot of Willow's bed as Jade grabbed the wand from the top of the dresser. Cass kept her eyes locked onto Skull Daddy's empty sockets as if he would wake and sound the alarm.

Given their previous attempts to remove Skull Daddy, they were alarmed at how easy the operation was. Neither one of them could sleep that night. Each creak and moan of the house had one or both of them shooting upright in bed, heart racing, wondering if this was the moment when they would be forced to face the consequences of their action.

But even with the toy taken out with the trash that night and hauled away by the garbage truck by the next morning, the hexing didn't stop. Less than a month later and they were still terrified of their six-year-old. No one left the house anymore.

Willow no longer needed a wand, and she didn't need to call out that she was performing a hex. Things broke when she laughed, they broke when she cried, and chaos reigned when she threw a tantrum. None of the incidents were coincidental.

And that wasn't the worst of it. One day, when Jade tried to stick her head out the back door to let Willow know her snack was ready, the door wouldn't budge. She fought with it, panicking as her skin stuck to the frame and blood slicked the handle. She ran to the kitchen window but couldn't open that either. She was still crying, tearing her fingernails out on the edges of the windowsill when Willow walked in from the backyard. When Jade approached the door, the blood was gone but the back door was still shut. She tried the front door next, but that too wouldn't open.

Not long after, Cass got a call from her boss. Her performance was failing, and although they assured her that they were sympathetic to her recent loss and health problems, they had no choice but to let her go.

Jade couldn't help but wonder if it was all a coincidence, or if Cass really had been missing too many deadlines at work. After their day at the mall, Willow appeared to have forgiven Cass. Maybe she wanted both of her parents to stay home with her all the time. Or maybe she and Skull Daddy had nothing to do with it. It was hard to shake the paranoia.

"We're being held hostage," Jade whined.

Cass placed her hands on her wife's shoulders and squeezed.

"We'll get through this." Nothing in her tone suggested she believed her own words.

"I tried contacting that psychologist again," said Jade. Her voice trembled. "My phone couldn't get a signal. No internet, no service. It's like *he* knew. And then when I went to order takeout, suddenly everything worked again. But I haven't been able to turn on my phone in a while. It doesn't stay charged anymore."

Cass nodded. She glanced over Jade's shoulder at the tarp-covered and broken kitchen window, and the collage of melted bowls fused to the stovetop.

"Yeah. I don't think Willow's the only one doing all this."

"We have to find a way to get rid of him," said Jade.

Her voice was so low that Cass could barely hear her. She looked down at her raw and bloody hands. Her skin was now peeling away in chunks and the remains of the Band-Aids from the first aid kit weren't helping to heal or protect her mangled flesh.

"But I can't get him off the wall. You know I've tried."

"Maybe we should call a priest. Not that we'd be allowed to use the phone." Jade chuckled, and the strained laugh made her sound like she was on the verge of hysteria. But she suspected she was well past the threshold.

Cass thought for a moment, biting her lip a little too hard.

"I'll try my computer. I haven't opened it in a while, so maybe he's forgotten it exists. We'll send out emails to different churches. CC them. Send them all at once so we can't be stopped after the first."

"Yes!" Jade checked herself, after realizing how loud she said that. "It's worth trying."

Cass tiptoed across the floor towards her laptop bag. She brought it into the kitchen and positioned herself at the island so that she was facing the door, just in case Willow or Hazel decided to come down the stairs. Jade stood close, almost touching Cass, as the screen lit up

Glancing at the door to the kitchen every few seconds, Cass drafted a letter and opened several tabs. She loaded the first ten church websites that popped up in her search and scoured the pages for email addresses, eyes darting back and forth as fast as they could. Without bothering to waste time with any unnecessary pleasantries or social etiquette, Cass double-checked only that she had included her contact information and home address in the email before pressing send.

The screen went grey, and a small notification appeared in the centre. It dutifully informed Cass that there was no internet connection. She tried refreshing the page, but she knew what the result would be. Nothing.

"Cass!"

Jade ran into the kitchen and filled a glass with water while Cass turned to look at the router in the living room. It was engulfed in flames. The wall behind it showed no signs of being singed, and the shelf it sat on was untouched, but the router itself was becoming a puddle of liquid plastic and wires. When Jade doused it with water, it continued to disintegrate until it no longer held any shape.

"Fuck," said Cass as she pulled out her phone, hoping in vain to use data to send the email that was now, in theory, waiting in her drafts.

With a pop, the phone jumped out of her hand and crackled as it hit the floor. It danced across the tile of the kitchen, like a fish flopping on the beach, as its innards exploded. Long after it stopped moving, Jade and Cass continued to stare at its charred shell.

"Mama!" came a singsong voice from upstairs.

Cass tensed.

"What is it, Willow?"

Jade held her breath, waiting for Willow to tell Cass that Skull Daddy was unhappy with her. Very, very unhappy.

"Can you bring me a snack?"

"What do we say, Willow?" Cass slapped her hands over her mouth. She regretted her response the second she said it.

It was force of habit she had been attempting to suppress. She could not risk angering her child.

Both women were frozen in place, holding their breath, and Cass began to tremble. She pressed her hands firmer over her lips to keep from screaming.

"Please," came a small, terse voice after a significant pause.

Cass looked at Jade with wide eyes, melting with relief. "Mommy and I will bring you up some apple slices."

Jade nodded. Neither one of them felt safe going up to their daughter's room anymore. But there was an illusion of safety in numbers.

"Mama?"

Cass's insides churned. She and Jade held their breath, waiting for the inevitable threat of punishment, lights dancing before their eyes.

"Can I have ice cream instead?"

"Sure." The word burst out of Cass with her breath. She gagged and choked back the bile that shot to the back of her throat. "You got it. Whatever you want."

"Thanks. Mama. I love you."

Cass swallowed hard. She reached for Jade's hand and squeezed.

"I... Mommy and I love you too, Willow."

September

"I understand," Jade said into her phone. Miraculously, it started working for this crucial task, but she knew that if she deviated from the plan – Skull Daddy's plan disguised as Willow's – the phone would die again, exploding like Cass's had. Jade was too tired – too scared – to argue.

She watched as blood and pus oozed out of every pore, every opening of her wife's body as the principal's voice droned on in her ear. She blinked, accepting the illusion as a threat, and Cass returned to normal. Well, as normal as she could look covered head to toe in a throbbing, red rash.

"Given what our family has been through these past couple of years – Yes, and that's why we decided homeschooling would be the best option for now. I – Yes, I understand school started last week, and this is last minute – Correct. Okay. Thank you. Yes, thank you."

She didn't get a chance to hang up. The phone did it for her seconds before it went black. Jade tapped the screen, the power button, the volume buttons, to see if there was any chance of bringing it back to life. There wasn't.

"There. It's done."

"Thank you," said Willow, taking the dead phone from her mother and gently placing it in the garbage. "I really don't feel like going to school anymore. I don't like the teachers, and the other kids are stupid and mean. Besides, Skull Daddy is teaching me."

"I'm sure he is," muttered Jade. She slumped into the couch and weakly reached for Cass's hand.

"Skull Daddy says it'll be better if he teaches me 'cause then I'll learn useful information. He says my talents would be wasted on the workforce," she said as if she was reading the information from a textbook or parroting what someone else had told her. She didn't struggle with any of the words, but it was clear she wasn't entirely certain what they all meant. "Adults grow old and die, and society chews them up and spits out their corpses. It's better to stay young and powerful forever. So that's what I'm gonna do. He's gonna teach me everything, and he and I are going to get everything we want from the world."

"Do you need anything else from us right now?" asked Cass. Her eyelids were drooping and she barely heard a word her daughter said. Jade's head was resting on her bony shoulder, and she too was on the verge of unconsciousness.

Willow thought for a moment. Her puckered little face would have been comical if her parents weren't terrified of her. "No. I'm going to go play in my room."

"Okay. Mommy and I are going to have a nap now."

"You need to kiss Skull Daddy goodnight first."

"No," moaned Jade, struggling to sit up. "No, we want to go back to bed."

Willow grasped both her mothers by the hands and squeezed harder than either of them thought was possible for a child.

"But you *have* to. Skull Daddy said he'll give you good dreams."

"I don't think that's what he's doing to us," whispered Cass.

Either Willow didn't hear her, or she ignored her mother outright.

"Mama, please. You have to. You don't want to hurt Skull Daddy's feelings."

Jade and Cass weren't sure if it was the result of another hex, the bone-chilling fear, or the overwhelming exhaustion they felt, but they allowed their daughter to lead them up to her bedroom.

Willow was still so small, yet she held herself like an adult, walking like Vera used to before arthritis and old age settled into her joints. She radiated confidence and control. Her mothers, by comparison, were cartoonish in their weariness. They stumbled up the stairs, skeletal, with excess flesh hanging off their bones as if someone had sucked out their insides through a straw. Cass's skin was bright red from the rash that coated her body, and Jade kept her free hand pressed firmly against her head to keep the unending headache from splitting it open. By the time they made it to the top of the stairs, both women were panting from the exertion as their daughter skipped across the landing to her bedroom.

Skull Daddy was waiting for them.

As the three of them approached the hollow-eyed presence that rested on the wall, Jade could have sworn that one of the bony sockets winked at her. Trembling, she leaned forward to kiss the smooth forehead, as she had done every day for the past few weeks at Willow's request. The warmth of the bone revolted her, and her nostrils filled with the smell of rot. As she pulled her lips away, she could feel that yet another piece of her had been left behind.

By the time it was Cass's turn, Skull Daddy was hot and small tendrils of steam crept out of the cracks and crevices. Cass was nauseous and lightheaded by the time she finished.

"Okay, you can go back to bed now," said Willow.

She followed her parents as they shuffled out the door and closed it behind them, watching their every move. While Hazel pawed at her feet, Willow listened for the sound of their own bedroom door closing before she went back to Skull Daddy with a smile.

Willow sat cross-legged on her bed, adjusting her skirt and pulling Hazel into her lap. As the cat began to purr, Willow looked up at the ram skull on the wall and chanted to it in a voice that was not her own.

"Skull Daddy, Skull Daddy, what do you see? What does the future hold for me?

Skull Daddy, Skull Daddy, what do you hear? Is it a friend or a foe that is near?

Skull Daddy, Skull Daddy, is it the time? The moment for me to claim what is mine?"

She paused and listened, hearing only the soft rumbling from Hazel and her own heartbeat. But Hazel stopped and lifted her head, ears perked up towards the skull. A deep, hoarse whisper floated out from between Skull Daddy's teeth.

Child of maiden, mother, crone, in this world of flesh and bone,

Visit me in darkest night and feed me with your shining light.
For helping me complete my task, I will grant you all you ask.

October

Willow hummed tunelessly to herself as she set up the plastic teacups the way Skull Daddy told her to. Everything had to be just right. It wasn't that she didn't want him to be mad – which was a more terrifying experience than she cared to admit – she *needed* to be perfect for him. He deserved it. Skull Daddy took good care of her.

"Like this?" she asked with childish enthusiasm.

Yes. Well done.

Willow beamed and scrunched the edges of her skirt in her fists.

Now the stones.

She hopped to her feet and skipped towards her hiding spot. Hazel stretched and yawned as Willow flung herself back down on the ground, jar in hand. It was filled with stones she found on the playground and in the backyard outside. Skull Daddy told her where to find them. He always told her where to find the best stuff.

She didn't think they were all fancy like her Mommy's amethyst crystal that sat at the bottom of the jar. Some were plain rocks that were fun shapes or had really smooth surfaces. And some had little sparkly flecks that danced in the light. Skull Daddy knew why they were important, and she trusted he knew what he was doing. He was a grown up, after all. And he was always right.

"What's this for again?" she asked as she placed a stone in each cup.

We're going to try a more complicated spell today. It will give both you and I more power, and– Not that one. The black one from the garden.

"This?"

She held it out to him. The skull on the wall did not nod, but she felt that's what he would have done if he had a proper body. He would soon though. That's what he kept telling her. Once his power was restored, he would get his body back. And then the two of them would get to go on an adventure.

Hazel was allowed to go with them, but not her parents. They couldn't do magic and had to stay behind. Willow would miss them, and promised to think about them every day. She would send them healing spells through her thoughts so that they could get better faster. She knew there was something about Skull Daddy that made grown-ups sick, but it couldn't be helped. He needed to get better too so he could get his body back, and Willow was happy to help.

"This is fun. I like this game."

I'm sure you do. You'll like tomorrow's game even more.

"What's tomorrow?"

It's a surprise.

Willow sulked but didn't dare pester Skull Daddy. She learned the hard way that doing so was not a good idea. He hurt her head when he was mad. Like the kind of hurt that happened when one of the kids she used to see at school hit her on the head when playtime got too rough. The kind of hurt that stayed for a long time and made it difficult to go to sleep. Besides, Skull Daddy always gave the best surprises.

Hazel stretched once more before padding out of the room to survey the rest of the house. Willow furrowed her brow as she watched her companion disappear into the darkness.

What is it?

"I just thought of something. What if Mommy and Mama get in the way again? What if they ruin things?"

Don't worry. It's already taken care of.

Willow nodded, relieved. It was exhausting trying to keep her parents from ruining her spells. Adults didn't understand. Skull Daddy said you had to learn magic when you were little. He learned it when he was little, and now he was super powerful and could do anything he wanted. Mommy and Mama never would have been able to do what Skull Daddy could. Not in a million years.

She let out a big sigh.

"I feel bad for them."

Why?

"Because they don't get it. They don't know enough about magic. They're too grown up and didn't get to learn it when they were little like you and me. And they're sad that Grandma's gone. I'm still a little sad too." She rocked the jar back and forth, watching the stones tumble over each other.

Don't be. Your grandmother is in a better world than this. And as for your parents, there's no need to worry about them. They're helping me, in their own way.

"Oh! They're helping you get your body back!" Willow clapped her hands together. Her smile filled her face at the thought of her parents being able to help Skull Daddy.

Yes, and they will be rewarded for their efforts. Mommy and Mama will see Grandma again soon.

"Oh really? That's great! Thank you, Skull Daddy. That'll make them all real happy. And I'm happy too!"

Excellent. I only want what's best for you. You know that, don't you?

"Of course!"

You're my favourite little apprentice. Your willful spirit makes you strong enough to withstand the toll magic takes on the body. And your determination has gotten me closer to freedom than I have ever been. All the children who came before you cannot compare.

Willow blushed. She wasn't sure what Skull Daddy was talking about, but she could tell he was pleased with her.

"I love you, Skull Daddy."

I know, child.

As Willow continued her work, following each of Skull Daddy's instructions as precisely as possible, Hazel made her way back up the stairs after completing her rounds. The house was secure. All the doors were bolted tight and the windows unmoving in their frames. There was a pile of accumulated flyers and envelopes in the front entrance, below the mail slot. Hazel batted at the papers as if they were her toys.

Before returning to her little human, she trotted over to the bedroom down the hall, the one with the door ajar. Without touching the door or frame, she slipped into the darkness. Only her eyes were visible as they reflected what little light there was. She scanned the room and took note of the situation. Her lips parted ever so slightly, revealing tiny fangs, and she tasted the strong scents that floated on the air. Everything was as the Master wished. Perfect.

Still, it never hurt to double-check. There was no telling how the Master would react if things did not go according to plan, and Hazel would never risk the safety of her little human, whom she loved above all else.

Without a sound, Hazel hopped up onto the bed. She was so light and agile that she barely disturbed the sweat-drenched sheets. Purring softly, she wove her way back and forth between the feet of the two humans. She bit into their toes to confirm what she already knew. They didn't move. Hazel's whiskers twitched at the intoxicating aroma of fresh death.

Satisfied that all was as it should be, Hazel returned to Willow's room. She rubbed her face against the child's back, but no more. She could not risk distracting her. Not now. Willow focused all of her attention on the carefully laid out cups and stones before her. She stared at them with dead, glassy eyes while muttering incantations taught to her by the Master.

Hazel sat upright at Willow's side, keeping her eyes fixed on the skull on the wall. Tendrils of smoke began to creep out of the cracks and crevices, billowing out of the eye sockets and nostrils. Hazel could feel the heat on her whiskers.

By the time the room was hazy with smoke and the skull was almost obscured, Willow sat a little straighter and the life came back into her eyes. Her face lit up with childlike wonder as the corners of her lips turned into a smile.

"He's coming."

Acknowledgements

I am so happy that I finally get to share this story with my readers. Over the past few months, I feel like *Skull Daddy* is all I've been able to think about. Other than cats, of course. This is one of my favourite stories to date, and I loved writing and editing it.

After a playdate with my youngest niece in the summer of 2021, I was inspired to write a dark little story based on what her parents told me about her favourite Halloween decoration. She called the thing Skull Daddy and kept it up on her bedroom wall long after Halloween was over. Yes, it's a black ram skull. And thankfully, it's made of plastic.

By February of 2022, I had a first draft of over 11,500 words. As I began my edits, I realized there was much more to this queer domestic horror story and I needed to write more. At one time, I even attempted to squeeze a novel out of it, but soon realized that a novella was a much more appropriate length.

Two years (and 11 drafts) later, I was ready to unleash *Skull Daddy* and share him with the world. What he does with his newfound freedom is his own business.

Thank you to my beta readers, my friends, and my husband for cheering me on. Thank you to my cats for reminding me to take breaks, and for adding extra "words" to my drafts. (Please stop stepping on my keyboard. Bubs, I'm looking at you).

Thank you to my writing buddy / neighbour / podcast co-host / friend Trevor for your honest feedback on multiple drafts. I'm glad I was able to make you uncomfortable again.

Thank you to Lisa Gilliam for the exceptionally thorough edits. And thank you to my friends Kat and Ama for giving me permission to create a story based on your delightfully strange child.

Of course, the biggest thank you of all goes to my niece Ivy. She created Skull Daddy; I just gave him a world to live in. And yes, she is the inspiration behind Willow, although she is much less dangerous.

I hope.

Don't miss out!

Visit the website below and you can sign up to receive emails whenever Stephanie Anne publishes a new book. There's no charge and no obligation.

https://books2read.com/r/B-A-IKLN-WUXCD

BOOKS 2 READ

Connecting independent readers to independent writers.

Also by Stephanie Anne

Watch for more at www.stephanieanneauthor.ca.

About the Author

Hello, readers! Thank you for stopping by. My name is Stephanie Anne and I am an oddball extraordinaire. My writing assistants include my cats Minerva, Finn, and Bubs. Unfortunately, they like to sleep on the job. I have a love for all things strange and monstrous and I hope you do to. If you like disturbing horror stories and unsettling tales of science-fiction, you've come to the right place.

Read more at www.stephanieanneauthor.ca.